CRUSHING ON MY DOCTOR

IONA ROSE

Hey there!

Thank you for choosing my book. I sure hope that you love it. I'd hate to part ways once you're done though. So how about we stay in touch?

My newsletter is a great way to discover more about me and my books. Where you'll find frequent exclusive giveaways, sneak previews of new releases and be first to see new cover reveals.

And as a HUGE thank you for joining, you'll receive a FREE book on me!

With love,

Iona

Get Your FREE Book Here:
https://dl.bookfunnel.com/v9yit8b3f7

Crushing on my Doctor

IONA ROSE

Crushing on my Doctor

Publisher: Some Books
978-1-913990-14-5

ERIKA

I pick my phone up when a text message pings in. I roll my eyes when I see who it's from. Jeremy. My ex-boyfriend. I broke up with him three days ago and since then, he's texted and called me constantly. It's ironic really because I think he's contacted me more in the three days we've been separated than he did in the full four months we were dating. And that's not because he ignored me while we were dating. It was just because while we were dating, he didn't show me this crazy, desperate stalker like side of himself.

I already know I won't be responding to his text message. I tried that with the first few messages I got off him after we had broken up. First I politely reminded him of why we had broken up and I told him multiple times that I didn't want to get back with him. After that kind of message being ignored several times, I resorted to telling him in no uncertain terms not to call or text me again. And when that didn't work, I just stopped responding. I blocked him on all of my social media accounts and I started to just ignore his calls and texts. And still, they keep coming. My God. There are some people who just can't take a hint. And then there's this.

Despite knowing I'm not going to be answering the message, I can't resist taking a peek at it. I roll my eyes again when I read it. Jeremy starts out by calling me "Baby" which I hate and he knows it. And the message only goes downhill from there.

"Baby, please just give me one more chance. I know you say it's over, but for me it will never be over. I miss you so much and I swear if you just agree to take me back, I'll be a better boyfriend. XXX"

The trouble is, there's nothing Jeremy can do to change my mind about this. I didn't end things with him because he was a bad boyfriend. I ended things with him because there was just no spark between us. He's a nice enough guy and we did have fun together in the beginning, but there was no chemistry between us, no magic or spark when we kissed. When I saw him, I didn't go weak at the knees or feel much of anything really. When we had sex, it was fine, but that was all it was. I don't want to spend my life having sex that's only fine with someone I like as a friend but nothing more. I want the real deal. And it seems pointless to drag our relationship out when I know for sure that Jeremy isn't the one.

Another text message pings in while I am reading the first one. Jeez. Give me a break. I read the next message. It's pretty much the same thing, only this time, Jeremy is pleading for me to answer the text message. He claims that he just wants to know that I'm ok, and if I say I still don't want to get back with him, he'll leave me alone. It feels like a trap. Like if I open communications with him again I'll be inviting him back into my life.

I tell myself that's stupid. If I tell him one more time we're done, then he'll have to accept it and then we can both move on. And if he still doesn't get the hint, then I'll just stop answering him once more and never get suckered into breaking my rule on that one again. I think for a moment and then I type out a response.

"I'm sorry Jeremy, what you feel I do not. It's over. Please stop contacting me and move on with your life."

It's short and to the point and there's no way Jeremy can read anything more into it than what's there. I nod my head in approval and send the message. It's barely left my phone when I hear another message ping in and I moan out loud in frustration. I laugh at myself when I see the name on the screen though. Jennifer. My best friend.

Her text message is much more welcome than Jeremy's.

"Drinks later? Carl will be here to keep the kids so I am freeee x."

I type back an instant yes. It's Sunday tomorrow so neither of us have to be at work and it'll be good to let my hair down and have some fun, something I don't feel like I've done enough off lately. I realise then that Jeremy and I rarely went out anywhere – we also seemed to be either at his place or mine. Yes, I definitely need a night out. And Jennifer and I are overdue a catch up. Since she had her second baby, we haven't gotten to see each other half as much as we used to. I get it, but it's great to know I'll be seeing her later on today.

Jennifer texts back quickly saying she'll pick me up around seven. I check my watch. It's barely even eleven am and I have a feeling it's going to be a long day now.

~

I am just starting to think about going to take a shower and starting to get ready for tonight when there's a knock on my door. I shake my head. I know Jennifer has a thing about always being early, but three hours early is a big thing, even for her. It's not so bad though. I can be ready in an hour if I push it and at least then I can stop itching to get out. I am practically skipping when I get to the front door and pull it open. My heart sinks when I see who is standing on my doorstep.

"Jeremy? What are you doing here?" I say coldly.

I really thought my last text to him had worked. He hadn't called or texted since I sent it. But clearly, he still isn't getting the hint.

He smiles at me, a lopsided smile and I realise from that grin and the slightly glassy look in his eyes that he's been drinking. That explains why he's got one hand pressed against the door jamb. He's probably trying to stop himself from swaying.

"Is that any way to greet a friend," Jeremy says with a wide grin, slurring his words.

"I …" I start.

"You said we could still be friends Erika. Did you mean it or not?" he says.

"Well sure," I reply. But I didn't mean the sort of friends that drop around each other's places unannounced and uninvited. "What's up?"

"I just wanted to see you," Jeremy says.

"Well you saw me," I grin, aiming for a light hearted tone but really just wanting Jeremy to leave.

"I need to talk to you," he slurs.

I open my mouth to tell him I've said everything I needed to say to him and that I was actually on my way out, but Jeremy pushes himself off the door jamb and pushes past me, entering my home. He walks down the hall as I stare after him in open mouthed surprise at his rudeness. He doesn't look back to see if I'm following him or not. He just goes off into the living room.

I shake my head and slam the door closed, following him into the living room where he stands in front of the couch, swaying slightly with nothing to hold on to.

"Look Jeremy this isn't a good time. I'm going out soon and I need to get changed," I say.

"Don't let me stop you," he says with a lecherous grin that makes my stomach turn over and not in a good way. Jeremy must see my expression change because he sighs. "God I was joking Erika. Lighten up."

I decide the quickest way to get him to leave will be to hear him out and then tell him yet again that we're over.

"Well I'm all ears. What do you want to talk to me about?" I say.

"About us obviously," he says, his tone implying that I'm the stupid one here.

"There is no us," I point out.

"Sure there is," Jeremy says, undeterred by the obvious fact that I want nothing to do with him. "There will always be an us. Stopping responding to my messages doesn't change what we have."

"I stopped responding to your messages because you weren't getting what I was saying Jeremy. And you're still not. We tried it. It didn't work. And I don't want to be with you. Please just accept that and move on."

"Baby, what can I do to make you change your mind?" Jeremy slurs.

"There's nothing you can do. It's over. Now please leave," I say.

"Leave? So you can go out and find someone to replace me? I don't fucking think so."

Jeremy's voice has changed. He's shouting loudly enough that I know my neighbours will be able to hear him. I just hope they're at work or out somewhere so I don't have the embarrassment of seeing them nudging each other next time I see them.

"Well?" Jeremy demands.

I don't know what he wants from me. It wasn't like he asked me a question I am going to answer. Jeremy sounds angry now, and when he glares at me, I feel suddenly afraid. He ignores me for the moment and walks towards my TV. He swipes out with one arm, knocking it from the cabinet and onto the ground where it smashes in to a thousand pieces.

"What the fuck?" I shout, anger over taking my fear for a moment.

Jeremy turns back to me, his face a mask of anger. I have never seen him looking like this before. He looks through me like I haven't spoken and then he begins to march around the room, throwing my ornaments to the ground and smashing my favorite lamp. He stomps on my coffee table until the legs give away and it crashes to the floor. I watch, my mouth open in shock as fear courses through me. He's lost his mind completely and I have to get him out of here before this goes even further.

"Do you know why I'm doing this Erika?" Jeremy demands.

"I … No," I say, unsure of what answer he is looking for, what answer will calm him down.

"I'm doing this to show you how serious I am about you. And that you can't just blow hot and cold on me. You responded to my message earlier, gave me hope that we had a future and then nothing all day," he says.

He isn't shouting now. I almost wish he would go back to shouting. This quiet, calm voice that thrums with anger is much more dangerous than the yelling.

"I told you we were over. How is that blowing hot and cold?" I say when it's clear Jeremy is going to just stand there and stare at me until I answer him.

It was the wrong answer. Rather than calm him down, it makes him madder. His face contorts and turns red and then Jeremy roars like an animal. He pulls the painting I have above my fireplace down off the wall and slams it down on the back of one of my armchairs. He slams it over and over until the canvas splits and then he throws it angrily away. He closes the gap between us in three long strides, his sway no longer as pronounced as earlier. I can tell he's still pretty wasted though. His pupils are huge and when he presses his face into mine to yell at me, I can smell the alcohol fumes radiating off him. I don't think he's even close to sober enough for me to be able to reason with him. I have to try though. I move backwards slightly, but he follows me. I open my mouth to say something, anything. Jeremy beats me to it though.

"Who the fuck do you think you are Erika? Why do you think you're too fucking good for me huh?" Jeremy screams. His face is almost purple now he is so angry. A vein pulses wildly out of control on his forehead. I have never seen Jeremy like this before and it's truly scary.

"Well? Why do you think you're too good for me?" Jeremy screams again, grabbing my upper arms and giving me a little but rough shake when I don't answer his question quickly enough for his liking.

How about because you think it's ok to smash my place up and then get in my face and yell? That's what I'm thinking but it's not what I say. I'm not that stupid. I need to calm Jeremy down before this gets even more out of hand, not make him madder.

"I never said that I was too good for you," I start.

It's true. I didn't. And I wasn't even thinking it until this moment.

"No but you were thinking it weren't you? Princess Erika, waiting for her knight in shining fucking armour to come and give her a fairy tale ending. Well guess what? He's not coming. Because if I can't have you, then no one can," Jeremy yells.

As he says it, he reaches out for me again, but this time, he doesn't grab my upper arms. This time is so much worse; his hands grab me around the throat. The hands that used to caress me so gently are now choking the life out of me and I have no idea how this whole thing escalated so quickly.

I can feel panic gripping me as I struggle to breathe or get free. Preferably both. Instead of both, I get neither. My airway is well and truly cut off, and Jeremy is far too strong for me to push away. Even without my head spinning and my lungs burning from the lack of oxygen, I think he would still have been too strong for me to push off me. I slap at the hands around my neck, but Jeremy just carries right on squeezing as though my slapping does nothing but tickle and my panic is nothing but amusing. I think that's the worst part. I can see the amusement in Jeremy's eyes as he chokes the life out of me.

Through the rushing of my own blood that I can hear in my ears, I think I can hear something else. A siren. And it is getting closer. Please let it be real. Please don't let it be a hallucination.

My suspicion about the siren is confirmed when Jeremy curses and lets go of my throat. It is just in time. Large black globules have begun to float in front of my eyes and I think another ten seconds and I would have lost consciousness. Another thirty seconds or so and I might have been dead.

I bend double, rubbing my hands over my throbbing neck and coughing and choking as I try to breathe through my agonizing, bruised throat. Each breath brings blessed relief and at the same time, angry hot agony. It's an odd mixture, one I don't much care for, but the relief wins over the agony and I keep gasping.

"You called the fucking cops on me?" Jeremy asks.

Even in my current state I can't help but notice that he sounds not only surprised but a little bit hurt too, like I am somehow the bad guy here. I shake my head quickly, ignoring the pain in my throat, and trying to keep the judgemental tone I want to use out of my voice.

"You would have seen me on the phone if I'd called anyone," I say.

My voice is a little raspy but it doesn't sound too bad. It is hard to believe that just seconds ago, I had really thought I was going to die. That Jeremy was going to crush my windpipe until I was dead.

"It must be one of your neighbors. Nosey bastards never could mind their own business," Jeremy says, again sounding like he is the victim here, being persecuted by my mean neighbours for no reason.

The sirens are so close now that the police can only be a block or two away at most. Jeremy is going to have to make the choice between staying and tormenting me and then being arrested, or leaving while he still has a shot at getting away.

Unfortunately for me, there is a third option for Jeremy. One I hadn't thought of. His fist flies out, catching me unaware. It catches me square in my cheekbone, a stinging blow that makes me take a step back. My foot catches on something and I stumble. I feel myself going down, my arms pinwheeling, looking for something to grab but finding nothing.

Jeremy has already turned and walked away from me, heading for the front door. I don't see whether he gets away or not, because as I fall, my head collides with the broken coffee table and everything goes black.

AIDAN

The ward seems to be particularly loud today as I make my rounds, checking on patient's charts and making sure all of their vital statistics are good, prescribing medications and writing a few discharge notes. I have just finished up the last bed when a nurse came towards me.

"Dr Miller, we have a new patient intake in room three. Would you mind taking a look at her?" she says.

"Sure," I agree. "What's her story?"

The nurse, Julie, looks down at a piece of paper she is carrying as we walk back down the corridor towards the private rooms at the end of the ward.

"Female, estimated to be in her early to mid thirties. She came in through the emergency room. She's unconscious but Dr Lowe from the emergency room is confident there is no skull fracture present after taking several x-rays. She has a bruise on her cheek bone and bruises around her neck consistent with being choked. An elderly neighbour heard commotion coming from her place so he called the police and when they arrived, they found the woman unconscious and her house trashed. The police called for an ambulance and she was brought here. The neighbor has told the police her name is Erika Hart and that's all we know at this time. The police are on standby and we're to call them when she wakes up and is up to being questioned about what happened to her," Julie says.

I blow out a low whistle.

"It sounds like she's been lucky to survive this. The police must have showed up at just the right moment to scare her attacker away," I comment. "Either that or they thought they had finished the job and left her for dead."

Julie nods her head.

"Yeah. Judging by the woman's neck, whoever did this to her meant business," she agrees.

We reach the room and I knock, just a habit really as I know the woman is unconscious. I open the door a crack and I hear a shrill alarm ringing out from the direction of the nurse's station. Julie glances down the corridor at the flashing red light indicating a patient is calling for assistance and then she glances at me.

"Go," I say to her. "I've got this."

She flashes me a grateful smile and hurries off to attend to whoever needs her. I push the door to the patient's room open a little further and step in. I move towards the bed as the door slowly closes behind me. I pick up the patient's chart and glance over it. It confirms everything Julie has just told me and nothing more. I didn't doubt that would be the case. Julie has been a nurse for a long time, and I swear she knows more about medicine than I do and she would never leave out an important detail on a patient's background when they're a new admission.

I glance up at the patient. She's lying on her back. A sheet is pulled up to her chest, her hands neatly folded on top of it. She's wearing a pink hospital gown. Her eyes are closed, her long eyelashes laid on her cheeks. I am meant to be looking at her neck, but I can't tear my eyes away from her face for a moment. This woman is gorgeous. Even the bruise on her cheekbone does nothing to diminish from her beauty. In fact, it makes her look vulnerable which somehow makes her even more attractive.

Her skin is pale and her long wavy hair is a natural looking red colour. Other than the bruise on her cheekbone, her face is unblemished, perfect. When I finally manage to tear my eyes away from the woman's face, I step closer and begin to look over her neck. The sight of the bruises there, obvious finger marks, make me feel sick. I am overwhelmed with a feeling of protectiveness for her, and I know if her attacker was before me right now, I wouldn't be able to stop myself from punching him. I swallow down my anger and gently put my hands on either side of the woman's neck, feeling for anything out of the ordinary. It all feels normal enough and I ignore the way her skin feels warm and delicious underneath my touch. I ignore the way it makes me feel like my hands are tingling. And I definitely ignore the way it makes my cock pulse with desire.

The woman makes a low moaning sound and her face screws up slightly as I probe at her injured neck. I take some of the pressure off, but I don't move my hands away fully; not yet. The woman's eyes open and I find myself looking into emerald green eyes, eyes so bright and vibrant that I want to look into them forever. She smiles at me and her beautiful eyes sparkle as she looks back into my eyes. I return her smile and we just stay that way for a moment, looking at each other.

"Who are you?" the woman whispers after a moment.

Her voice, her words, pull me out of this stupor I have found myself in and I straighten up, taking my hands from the woman's neck. Somehow, I miss the feel of her skin. I clear my throat, a little embarrassed that I have let myself act like this around a patient. At least her question didn't sound like she is afraid of me. Instead, she sounded curious, relaxed, like maybe she knew she could trust me. I tell myself I'm being silly and I smile at the woman.

"My name is Dr Miller," I say. "You're at Claremont Hospital. Do you remember what happened to you?"

"I … No," she says, screwing her face up slightly as she tries to remember.

She starts to push herself into a sitting position and I put my hand on her shoulder, gently holding her in place. I feel sparks running through my hand and up my arm where I touch her. She makes a soft gasping sound at my touch and I dare to let myself think that maybe she felt it too.

"Don't try to sit up just yet," I say with a smile, ignoring the sensation touching her gives me. "You were unconscious. I just need to check for a concussion."

I pull a little penlight from the pocket of my white coat and shine it in each of her eyes in turn. The light picks up flecks of gold in the green and I feel my insides stirring, desire flooding me. I force myself to ignore the feelings, concentrating on her pupils. They dilate normally and I smile at her, putting the penlight away.

"Your reaction times are fine," I smile. "And I would say it's unlikely you have a concussion, but we'll keep you in for a while just to be on the safe side. If you start to feel sick or dizzy, let a nurse know immediately."

She nods her head and I sit down on a chair I pull up to the side of her bed.

"What's your name?" I ask.

"Erika. Erika Hart," she says.

That's a good sign. She knows who she is. I run through the address details, the date of birth, and the medical history the system had linked to the tentative ID we had been given and everything matches what is on the chart. It doesn't seem like she's any the worse for wear for the bang she's taken on her head. The small cut she sustained has already been stitched and I'm confident that's the only damage that's been done to her head.

I run through a few more questions. What year it is, who is the president of the United States. I ask her where she went on her last holiday and she smiles at me.

"Greece. But how will you know if that's correct or not?" she asks.

"I don't," I confess. "But it's a test to see if you can answer questions quickly or if you have to really think about the answers."

"So what's the verdict? Am I broken?" she asks.

"Nope. You're as good as new," I say.

She blushes slightly and I feel my heart skip a beat. I can't let myself be attracted to this woman. It's unprofessional and she's been through enough without me coming on to her. I stand up and smile at her.

"One of the nurses will be along shortly to give you some pain meds for your neck. There doesn't seem to be any real damage done, but it will be sore for a few days until the swelling goes down," I say.

I head for the door.

"Dr Miller?" Erika says from behind me. She sounds unsure of herself suddenly and when I turn back to her, I see the fear on her face. "What happened to me? And why can't I remember it?"

I go back to the chair beside her bed. I was hoping I wouldn't have to be the one to have this conversation with her. I was hoping I wouldn't have to be the one to tell her that some monster had attacked her in her own home. But I can't bring myself to walk away from that pleading tone, the scared looking eyes.

"Call me Aidan," I say, something I always tell my patients. Dr Miller sounds so formal and patients are much more likely to open up to me in a less formal setting. "What's the last thing you remember?"

She thinks for a minute and then she nods slowly.

"I was meant to be going out on Saturday night. It is still Saturday right?" she says.

I nod my head.

"Yeah. Six o'clock Saturday night," I say.

"Right. I was meant to be going out with my best friend. I think it was about four, but I decided to start getting ready. More to pass the time than anything else really. I remember someone knocking on my door. And the next thing I remember is this," she says. "Was Jennifer early? Did we go out somewhere and have an accident? Is she ok Dr Mill … Aidan?"

Erika's voice is starting to sound panic filled and I shush her before she can work herself up into a frenzy.

"Your friend wasn't with you," I say quickly. "We don't know who was at your door, but one of your neighbours called the police because he heard a commotion coming from your place. When the police got there, they found you unconscious and the room around you trashed."

"Someone did this to me?" Erika says, her eyes opening wider.

"Yes. I'm sorry," I say.

"Who? Why?" she asks.

I wish I could take the fear out of her and make her feel like everything is going to be ok. Instead, I have to settle on the truth.

"I don't know," I say. "But the police want to come and talk to you and I'm sure they'll get to the bottom of it all."

I wasn't sure of that at all. How could they have any hope of finding out the truth about who had attacked her when Erika had no memory of what had happened?

"I definitely want to talk to them," Erika says. "But I don't know what I'll be able to tell them. They probably know more about this whole thing than I do."

"Maybe something they say will trigger something," I say, not really believing it but wanting to. Whoever did this to Erika needs to be caught and locked away.

"Why don't I remember the attack?" she asks.

"It could be one of two things," I say. "Either your mind has blanked out whatever happened because it's too traumatizing to remember. Or it could be a short term memory loss brought on by your head wound."

"But the memory will come back right?" Erika says.

"It could," I say. "But there's no guarantee it will. The odds are around fifty-fifty."

"Ok. Thank you," she says with a smile.

I know she's not really thanking me. I haven't told her what she wanted to hear at all. But it's the thing most patients say to doctors at some point, even when they're getting bad news. I smile and stand up again.

"If you're sure you're feeling up to it, I'll call the police and tell them you're ready for them," I say.

Erika smiles and nods.

"Will you call Jennifer too please? My best friend? She'll be so worried if she gets to my place and sees the mess and I'm not there," Erika adds.

"Of course," I say. I hand her a notepad out of my pocket and give her my pen. "Just write her number down on there."

Erika takes the pen and paper and flashes me a quick smile and then she scribbles down Jennifer's number.

"Has anyone called my parents? Do you know?" she asks.

I shake my head. Presumably we do not have any contact info given that we had little ID on her. If they had, it would have been in her chart.

"We like to get a positive ID from the police on people in these circumstances before we call their next of kin. Your neighbor told the police your name and they matched it to the address you were transported from, but we would have needed to be certain before we called anyone. I see we don't have a number contact for any family yet. If you want to jot the number down I'll call them now for you," I say.

"No," she says quickly. She smiles again. "Ok, that made it sound like we have some deep, dirty family history didn't it?"

"A little," I laugh.

"My parents live in Argentina. And that call would do nothing but worry them. They'd insist on flying out here and no amount of me telling them I was fine would stop them. I'm thirty-four, not twelve, and while I appreciate that they would only be doing it because they care, there's nothing they could do really and I'm ok," Erika explains.

She's thirty-four. Her date of birth told me that much of course, but looking at her face, I find it hard to believe all the same. There are no fine lines, no crinkles around her eyes or mouth. If I had had to guess her age, I would have said she was no older than twenty-seven.

"Well at thirty-four, I'd say you're old enough to make that decision for yourself. Let me just make a note in your chart so no one else notices they haven't been called yet and wants to make the call."

I hold my hand out and she looks at me, confused for a moment, and then she realizes she still has my pen. She gives me it along with Jennifer's number and her fingers brush mine as she does. Her cheeks flush slightly and she looks away from me quickly. She's definitely feeling the same spark I am feeling, but it doesn't matter. She's my patient. Nothing can happen between us.

I grab her chart and write down what she said about not informing her parents of her stay in hospital though she hasn't provided any number for anyone to do so. I replace her chart. I should leave now, go and call her friend and the police and then get on with my job, but I don't want to. I don't want to leave her here alone.

"Can I try sitting up now? I'm really thirsty," Erika says.

Is she trying to find a reason for me to stay? I hope so, but I tell myself I'm being ridiculous, looking for something that isn't there and something that I can't act on even if it is there. I nod my head.

"Slowly," I say.

I walk around the bed and help her into a sitting position.

"Do you feel dizzy or anything?" I ask.

"No," she replies.

She starts to reach for the jug of water on the cabinet beside her. I get to it first and pour some water into a plastic cup and hand it to her. She sips the water and makes an "ahh" sound. When she finishes the water, I take the cup back from her and refill it. Her lips are shiny, the water coating them and I feel an urge to lean in and kiss that water off her. I step back quickly before I can do something I will regret.

The door opens and I feel myself blushing red, although I have done nothing to warrant it. I thought about it, but I didn't actually do it. Erika looks equally flustered as Stacy, one of the nurses, steps into her room. She looks at Erika then at me and then she frowns. God, is it that obvious I was just thinking about kissing a patient?

"There you are," Stacy says. "Kevin has been looking all over for you."

"Kevin?" I say stupidly, just relieved she doesn't seem to have noticed the awkward moment she has disturbed.

"You know, Kevin, one of the nurses?" Stacy says. "Dr Miller are you ok? You seem a little off color."

"I'm fine," I say, back under control and cursing myself for not knowing who Kevin was. He's been a nurse here for a few months. I should know his name. I would have known his name if I wasn't so consumed by the wetness of Erika's lips. "What does Kevin want?"

"Mrs Adelman's scan was scheduled for like ten minutes ago," Stacy says. "He wants you to, you know, do the scan."

I smile, a smile that says I have got this.

"Yes of course. I hadn't forgotten about that." I am lying. I had forgotten about it. "I was just doing a preliminary exam on Ms Hart and she woke up."

"I can take over that for you," Stacy says, nodding to the trolley she's pulled into the room behind her with the blood pressure cuff, the oxygen monitor and the thermometer.

"Thank you," I say. "And can you call the police and let them know Ms Hart is ready to talk to them. Also, can you call this number? Ms Hart's friend was due to be picking her up from home at seven and she needs to know where she is."

I hand Stacy the paper with the number on it and she nods. She steps closer to Erika.

"How are you feeling Ms Hart?" she asks.

"Call me Erika," Erika says with a smile. "Sore but not too bad."

Stacy starts to apply the cuff to Erika's arm.

"I can give you some medicine for the pain if you need it. It has been prescribed for you," she says. She looks up at me. "Dr Miller? The scan?"

"Yes. Yes, of course," I say, and I rush from the room before I can make myself look any more useless.

ERIKA

To say the last couple of hours have been strange would be an understatement. First of all, there's the fact I was attacked brutally enough to leave me with a necklace of bruises and another bruise on my cheekbone. Plus, the cut on my head and the ache inside of my skull, which I have been assured is normal and the painkillers Stacy gave me are helping with that.

I have no idea who attacked me or why. And my memory of the whole thing is just gone. Like I told Dr Miller, Aidan, I remember deciding to go and get ready and then someone knocking on my door. And that's all I remember until I woke up in hospital. My mind is spinning with questions about the incident. Did the person who knocked on my door attack me? Or was that something innocent and then I did something stupid like forgetting to lock the door and someone came in after that? I know by the clothes in the cabinet beside my bed that I hadn't showered at the point of being attacked, because the clothes are the same jeans and t-shirt I was wearing on the Saturday afternoon.

And if all of that wasn't odd enough, then there's Aidan. I woke up from unconsciousness with no idea what had happened to me or where I was. I woke up to find myself looking into the eyes of a stranger, his hands on my throat. I should have been terrified, but I wasn't. His touch was gentle, his dark blue eyes were warm and caring, and somehow, I felt safe. When he stepped back and I got a good look at him, for a moment, I thought it was all a dream. It didn't seem possible that someone so good looking could exist in reality.

It's an understatement to say that Aidan is hot. His eyes are the color of the sea on a stormy day, dark blue and deep. When he smiles, they light up and twinkle and he has the cutest little dimples in his cheeks. He definitely works out. Even through the loose white coat I could see the muscles in his arms, on his chest.

The really weird thing is I don't think I'm the only one who felt the sparks flying between us. I really think Aidan felt it too. I am sure he was trying to find excuses to stay longer in my room. I mean do doctors usually do the phone calls and pour water for patients? And when Stacy came in, I felt like she had interrupted an intimate moment somehow. Maybe the pain meds are just affecting my brain.

And now, as if that isn't all enough to make today a strange day, I'm sitting up in bed in a flimsy pink hospital gown that totally clashes with my hair and makes me look even paler than I am, waiting for the police to come and talk to me about me being the victim of a crime I don't remember. I hope someone has told them I don't remember anything. I don't want them to come in here expecting answers and instead get nothing. Because that's really all I have for them.

I'm pulled out of my musings by a beeping sound, which I realize is my text message alert on my phone. It must have been brought in with me. It was likely in my jeans' pocket. I swing my legs out of the bed waiting for a rush of dizziness that doesn't come. My neck hurts a little more as I bend down to the bottom drawer of the cabinet, but it's nothing I can't handle.

I pull the drawer open and lift up my jeans. I feel the pockets and find I was right. My phone is in the pocket. I smile to myself as I fish it out. I put my jeans back away and close the drawer and get settled back into bed and then I read the message. It's from Jennifer.

"Oh my God. Just heard what happened to you. Are you alright? X"

I type out a response assuring her that I'm fine and telling her that I don't really know what happened to me. She texts back asking if she can come and see me during visiting hours tomorrow. I instantly text back telling her yes, that would be great.

I look through my texts to see if I've missed any others. There's one from a few hours ago, Jennifer telling me how much she's looking forward to our night out. I feel a little bit guilty about that, but it's hardly like I'm just flaking out on her. I notice there are no more texts or calls from Jeremy and I smile. At least one good thing has come out of today. It must have really worked when I sent the last text to him and told him one more time we were done.

A knock sounds on my room door and I slip my phone into the top drawer of the cabinet which I can reach without having to get out of bed.

"Come in," I call, surprised that the nurse has waited for me to invite her in.

The door opens and I see why. It isn't a nurse. It's two police officers. One is a short black woman with her hair scraped back into a neat little bun. The other one is a tall male officer. He doesn't look old enough to be out of high school. I tell myself that's a sure fire sign that I'm getting old. The female officer steps forward and extends her hand. I shake it.

"My name is Officer Prescott and this is Officer Moore," she says. The male officer nods to me from the corner of the room where he's collecting two plastic chairs and bringing them to my bedside. "One of the nurses called and said you were ready to talk to us. Is that true?"

"Yes," I say, nodding my head. "But I really don't know how much use I can be. Did the nurse tell you I have no memory of the event?"

"She did," Officer Prescott smiled. "But that doesn't mean you can't tell us anything useful. You'd be surprised how many little things people think aren't important that actually are."

"Ok," I reply, nervous suddenly.

What if I don't tell them the little detail that can make a difference?

"What is the last thing you remember?" Officer Prescott asks me.

"I stood up to go and get a shower and get changed. I think it was around four o'clock. There was a knock on my front door, and that's the last thing I remember before waking up here," I tell her.

26

She just listens, nodding encouragingly, while Officer Moore takes notes of what I'm saying.

"What do you remember about the knock on the door?" Officer Prescott asks.

"What do you mean?" I say.

"Was the knock particularly loud or did it sound urgent? Anything like that?"

"Not that I can remember," I say.

"And do you remember having any ideas who it could be?"

"I thought maybe it was Jennifer. She's my best friend. We were going out that night and I thought maybe she had arrived early. I know that sounds crazy, but Jennifer has a habit of turning up early for everything. It wasn't her though."

"You remember it not being her?" Officer Prescott asks me.

"Not specifically, but she's my best friend. She wouldn't attack me or trash my house," I say with confidence.

"Don't worry," Officer Moore put in. "Your friend isn't a suspect. She has an iron clad alibi for the time of the attack. We're only asking these questions in case they trigger something."

"You checked Jennifer's alibi? As in she was a suspect at one time?" I ask, surprised.

"Not so much of a suspect as someone to eliminate from our investigation," Officer Prescott says with a smile. "Are you in the habit of letting strangers into your home Ms Hart?"

"No, of course not," I reply.

"There was no sign of forced entry and no sign of a struggle in the hallway. This could indicate that your attacker was someone you knew," she said.

"I thought of that," I admit. "But I also thought maybe it was someone I knew at the door, or a salesman or something, and then maybe I forgot to lock the door after me. I don't think I've ever done that before, but never say never right."

Even as I say it, I know that's an unlikely scenario, but is it any more unlikely than thinking someone I knew well enough to invite inside my home would do this to me?

"That's also possible and we'll be checking the nearby area to see if there are any CCTV cameras close enough to maybe have picked something up. You don't happen to have any cameras installed at home do you?" Officer Prescott says.

"No," I say. I think for a minute. "You think this is personal don't you?"

"It does look that way," Officer Prescott admitted. "But it could just have been an opportunist burglar who saw a chance to rob your house, however it is quite rare for a burglar to trash a room such as occurred in your house unless they are after something of particular high value and they won't usually hurt someone unless you could identify them. Whether either of these situations is relative we will obviously need you to go through your things and confirm nothing is missing, but on first glance it doesn't appear that you have been robbed. Your TV is still there though damaged and there's a laptop and jewellery sitting out in plain view in your bedroom. Your purse wasn't touched either. There is of course still a chance that this was a burglary and that the police arrived quickly enough to scare the person off without them having time to take anything. But harming you is still puzzling were that the case"

"Do you know of anyone who might want to harm you Ms Hart? Anyone who dislikes you or who you've had a run in with recently?" Officer Moore puts in, his pen poised ready to note down my answer.

I think for a moment. I don't for a second think everyone in my life adores me, but I really can't think of anyone who hates me enough to do this to me. I shake my head.

"Not that I can think of. I mean I get on reasonably well with all of my colleagues and I haven't been sleeping with anyone's boyfriend or anything if that's what you're think-ing," I say, smiling to show I'm at least partially joking about that last part.

Officer Prescott returns my smile but it doesn't meet her eyes.

"Be honest with me Officer. What are the chances of you catching this guy?" I ask.

"We have two officers on the scene right now. They are collecting finger prints and DNA evidence from the scene. Chances are most of the samples will be yours. We will have you come down to the station once you're feeling better and give us a DNA sample and take your finger prints so we can eliminate those. If we find any other samples, then we will try to find a match in our database. You will also need to provide a list of current relationships, any boyfriends past and current, acquaintances and any other potential persons we can look into. If the crime was an opportunist, then there's a chance they'll be in the system having done this before and then we'll catch him. If it turns out to be personal, and the person who attacked you doesn't have a record, then honestly, the chances of finding him are quite slim. There is also the possibility that you will regain at least some memory of the incident which could be invaluable to catching the person."

"Like I said, we'll be looking for any CCTV of the area and we'll be going door to door to talk to your neighbors, but it's not a lot to go on."

I nod my head. It's pretty much what I expected to hear. Another thought comes into my mind.

"What will happen to my house? I mean is it left unlocked?" I say.

"The officers on the scene collecting the evidence will secure the property when they leave and you will be able to collect your keys from the station whenever you're ready," Officer Prescott says.

"Thank you," I say. "Officer, should I go back? What's the chances of this guy, whoever it is and whatever motive he had to hurt me, coming back to finish the job?"

"I would say that's unlikely, but I wouldn't like to say with one hundred percent certainty that won't be the case. If you have someone you could stay with for a short time until we conclude the investigation, that might be for the best," Officer Prescott said.

"In other words, wait long enough for him to realize he's gotten away with this and then hope he's clever enough to take the win and stay the hell away from me?" I say.

"Pretty much, yeah," Officer Prescott says, surprising me with her honesty.

My surprise must show on my face because she goes on.

"I know that is a little disheartening, but it's the truth Ms Hart and I don't want to mislead you. Please don't think we aren't taking this seriously though because we are. I promise you we will do our best to catch your attacker."

"There's just not much to go on at this stage of the investigation," I finish for her.

"Exactly," she says. She digs in her pocket and hands me a small card. "Here's my card. If you do start to remember anything about the attack, even if it seems small or insignificant, give me a call ok? Remember that nothing is totally insignificant and no matter how small a detail something seems to be it could turn out to be important."

I nod my head and she smiles again and then stands up. Officer Moore puts away his notebook and stands up too. He gathers the chairs and takes them back to the corner.

"Once you are released, please do let us know where we can find you Ms Hart," Officer Prescott says as they head for the door.

"I will. Thank you Officers," I say.

I lean back against my pillows and sigh. They have as good as told me that they're not going to be able to find whoever did this to me. So that leaves me with two options. I can lay here and feel sorry for myself, or I can put the attack behind me and get on with my life. I choose option B. I decide the first thing I have to do is to take a look at my face and neck. I want to see how bad the damage is.

I slowly get up out of bed, pleased to note that there's still no rush of dizziness. The movement makes the pain in my head a little bit worse, but it's nothing I can't handle. I walk slowly to the small bathroom in my room and approach the sink. I keep my head held high, needing to see how bad I look before I change my mind about looking.

To be honest, I was expecting it to be worse than it is. I had blown it up out of all proportion in my head, imagining a Frankenstein's monster style nightmare of stitches. I don't know why – the only stitches I have are the ones in the back of my head. Maybe I'm crazy as well as bruised.

There's a smallish bruise on my cheekbone that annoyingly looks like a smudge of dirt due to the dark colour of it. I discovered it was a bruise when I tried to wipe it off and found the spot tender. My neck is a mess of bruises, some clear fingerprints sitting darker against the yellowish tinge of the entire area. It makes me shudder to think how close I seem to have come to being choked to death and catching my attacker seems to be way down a long list of crimes for the police. Stacy, the nurse who was here earlier, even told me I was lucky that my windpipe hadn't been crushed.

Overall, I have looked better yes, but it's not that bad. And it's not like anything will permanently scar. Actually, my head wound might. I don't know how deep the cut was. But nothing that is visible will permanently scar. If it's possible to have your home broken into and vandalized and to be physically assaulted and still be classed as lucky, then yes. I guess I am lucky.

I hear the door to my room open and I leave the bathroom. Aidan is back and I smile at him, feeling a tingling sensation in my clit when he returns my smile. I love that I've gotten to meet Aidan, but I hate how it happened. I mean talk about embarrassing. I can only hope I wasn't drooling while I was unconscious. And the hospital gown is doing nothing to make me feel better about the way I look.

"How are you feeling?" Aidan asks me.

"Better," I smile. "The nurse gave me some painkillers which have taken the throbbing in my head down to more of an irritable ache. And I've just taken a look at my neck and it's not quite as hideous as I imagined it was going to be."

"Nothing about you is hideous," Aidan says.

He blushes as he says it and then he clears his throat, looking away from me and grabbing my chart. I bite my bottom lip to stop myself from smiling. This attraction I am feeling is definitely not one-sided.

"Everything looks in order here," Aidan smiles at me. "Assuming everything stays like this, I can see no reason why you shouldn't be home within the next couple of days."

"I don't know if that's a good idea," I blurt out before I can stop myself.

Aidan frowns slightly and drops my chart back in its holder and then he comes to sit down on the side of my bed. He faces me and I am aware of how close his body is to mine. I can feel the heat coming off him even through the sheets. I can feel my pussy starting to dampen as I imagine reaching out and pulling him closer, him slipping beneath the sheets with me.

I want to shift positions slightly so that I'm even closer to him, but I'm scared that if I move I'll spook him and he'll jump back away from me.

"Why not? Did the police say something about who did this to you?" he asks.

I shake my head.

"Not exactly. In fact, I'm confident they won't find the person who did it which is what is worrying me. They said that the chances of my attacker returning are slim, but I'm not sure I want to take that risk you know."

"I don't want to worry you further Erika, but I actually think it might be a good idea if you find somewhere temporary to stay until everything quietens down," Aidan said.

It was basically what the police had said. Give the guy time to realize he had gotten away with the attack and then hope he was smart enough to take that as a win and stay away from me. It made me angry that everyone seemed so sure he would get away with it, but I couldn't fault the logic of it. I couldn't remember anything and that meant the police had nothing to go on.

"I think you might be right," I say, forcing myself to smile although I'm a little worried about where I will go. I will worry about that later. Aidan said I have a day or two in here before I have to start thinking about that.

He stands up and smiles down at me.

"My shift is about over and I just wanted to check in on you before I finished for the night. I'll be back in tomorrow, and the doctor who is working tonight is very good so don't worry," Aidan said.

"I won't," I smile. "Goodnight."

"Goodnight Erika."

I wait until he's almost out of the room before I'm brave enough to ask what I want to ask.

"Aidan?" I say.

He turns back to me.

"Do you go around and say goodnight to all of your patients like this?" I ask, a flirty smile on my lips.

Aidan returns my smile and shakes his head.

"No. But none of them have ever had an effect on me like you have Erika."

He leaves quickly before I can even begin to respond to that. My stomach feels warm and swirly and my pussy aches for Aidan's touch. Hearing that I am having a similar effect on him is both reassuring and exciting.

I think I'll have a hard time sleeping tonight, thoughts of the attack and visions of Aidan stopping me from switching off my brain. I am wrong though. I drift off to sleep almost as soon as Aidan leaves the room.

I wake up to a light tapping sound on my room door. It takes me a moment to remember where I am, and as soon as I do, the throbbing pain in my head starts up again.

"Come in," I croak.

I clear my throat and push myself into a sitting position as Officer Prescott comes into my room. I frown in surprise. I hadn't expected to see her so soon.

"Is everything alright?" I ask.

Officer Prescott nods and smiles.

"Yes, everything's fine," she says. "But the team from your home have managed to identify two different strands of DNA in your living room right around where the attack took place. We believe one to be yours, but we really need to be certain just so it can be eliminated from the investigation before we cross match the sample with our records. I wondered if you would be willing to provide a sample of your DNA now?"

"Yes. Yes, of course," I reply after taking a moment to consider if this is good news. It probably wasn't. Unless the guy was a repeat offender, it wouldn't help because his DNA wouldn't be on their files if he hadn't done anything wrong before. "Do you need me to call the nurse to take the blood?"

"It's nothing that drastic. Just a cheek swab," Officer Prescott smiles. She opens a small packet she's pulled out of her bag and hands me what looks like a long cotton Q-tip. "Just rub that on the inside of your cheek and pop it in the bag."

I do as she says and hand the bag back to her. She seals the top and drops it back in her bag.

"Have you remembered anything about the attack?" she asks looking at me hopefully.

I shake my head, feeling like I'm somehow letting her down. She smiles sadly and squeezes my shoulder before she turns to leave. I watch her retreating and right at the last second, I think of something and call out to her.

"My keys. You said I could pick them up from the station. Is it ok to send someone else to pick them up on my behalf? I need some things for while I'm in here," I say.

Officer Prescott nods.

"Sure. That's fine. Who will it be?"

"Jennifer Palmer," I say.

Officer Prescott nods again and leaves the room. I text Jennifer, realizing now that I probably should have asked her to do this before I said it. It doesn't matter. Jennifer responds quickly saying of course she'll pick up my keys and some things for me. I send her a list of what I need. Clothes. Clean underwear. Pajamas. A towel. Toiletries. My phone charger. That kind of thing.

I hate the fact that I can't even shower or brush my teeth until Jennifer gets here, but it's not like I have any real choice in the matter. I lay back against my pillow and close my eyes, knowing I won't sleep, but hoping I can anyway. It will pass the time.

❧

It's fair to say Jennifer is an absolute legend. Within an hour of me texting her, a nurse tapped on my door and brought in my familiar pink overnight bag. She told me someone had dropped it off for me. I smiled my thanks and opened it quickly. On the top was a note from Jennifer; I thought you might like this stuff now rather than waiting until visiting hours.

She was so right. I went through everything and then I went and had a nice hot shower and washed my hair and brushed my teeth. Clean and dressed in my own clothes again, I actually felt something like a human again.

Jennifer is back now. She came back during visiting hours just like she said she would. I have been updating her on everything that's happened and what the police have had to say about it all.

"So I still don't know whether or not I should go home. The police hinted at me maybe not going back for a while but didn't sound overly convinced I wasn't just being paranoid. But my doctor agreed it was a good idea. Staying away for a while I mean."

"Yes, he's right. I think you should find somewhere else for a while too," Jennifer says without hesitation.

"You're that sure my attacker will come back?" I ask, shocked and a little frightened.

"No," Jennifer says quickly, shaking her head. "But I can see you're frightened to go back there and you need someone to tell you not to. If you go back, you're only going to be on edge, looking over your shoulder constantly."

I nod my head. She's right.

"Yeah. I should probably look for a hotel room or something," I say.

"You know I'd offer to let you stay with us, but right now, I don't even know where I'd put you," Jennifer says.

I shake my head quickly.

"Don't be silly. I'll find something," I say.

I get why Jennifer can't put me up and I never expected her to even offer. Jennifer is still in the middle of moving. Her family has had to downsize after her husband, Carl, lost his job. There are now four of them – Jennifer, Carl and their two children - crammed into a tiny, one bedroom apartment. There's no way I'd make that uncomfortable living situation any worse by asking to stay with them.

We talk for a bit longer and then the bell sounds to inform us that visiting hours are now over. It sure doesn't feel like it's been two hours, but a quick glance at my watch, a watch Jennifer thought to bring me, tells me it has been. We say our goodbyes and Jennifer leaves after hugging me tightly.

I pick up my phone and open up Google and search for hotels in my local area. I am horrified to see the prices. Even the cheap ones are upwards of one hundred dollars a night. My few savings will be gone within a week or two at that rate and that's without food or anything. It's not even like I'll have any money coming in.

The door opens while I'm considering hostels instead. Aidan smiles at me and I return the smile, putting my phone down on the bed beside me.

"How are you feeling?" Aidan asks me.

"Ok," I say.

"You don't sound ok. You sound worried," he says, a frown of concern on his face.

I shake my head and sigh.

"I'm looking for a hotel room to stay in for a while just until I feel safe to go home. But they're all out of my price range. So

IONA ROSE

now I'm thinking I might have to stay in a hostel and I'm not exactly relishing the idea," I tell him.

"Have you considered renting a room?" he asks.

"What like in someone's apartment?" I ask.

He nods and I shake my head.

"I know this is going to make me sound crazy and paranoid, but I just know that with my luck, I'd be the unlucky one who ended up living with some massive psycho type," I say.

Aidan laughs softly.

"You sound like my sister. Actually, there's an idea," he says.

I look at him questioningly and he explains.

"My sister has just graduated from college and she moved into an apartment. She was thinking of getting a roommate but she's a lot like you. Paranoid about the sort of person she might end up living with. I could call her and see if you could take the room for a few weeks if you want me to?" Aidan says.

I think for a second. Is it a good idea? I mean the chances of Aidan's sister being a psycho who wants to kill me are slim. And I like the fact she thinks the same way as I do. I also like the fact that maybe this means Aidan wants me to stick around in his life once I'm out of the hospital.

Aidan is looking at me strangely and I realize I've been quiet for too long. He probably thinks I'm going to say no and that he's scared me off or something. I smile at him and nod my head.

"That would be great," I say. "Thank you."

40

Aidan smiles at me again and he starts towards the door.

"I'll go and call her now," he says.

I watch his ass as he slips out of the door. It's a nice ass. One I really want to get my hands on. Maybe my mouth on as well. I try not to get my hopes up though. Either about Aidan's ass or about the room. I could be reading far too much into his offer to call his sister. I mean it's not just me he's helping, it's her as well and it makes sense that he would want to help his sister. And as for the room, there's no guarantee Aidan's sister will say yes. I mean if she's worried about living with a stranger, then Aidan's call isn't going to help much. It's not like I'm a friend of his who he's known long enough to vouch for. I'm a patient who he has known for all of five minutes.

ERIKA

I don't have to wait long to find out whether or not Aidan's sister is willing to risk me being a nut job and let me stay in her spare room. Aidan comes back to my room within ten minutes of leaving it. And he's beaming.

"She said yes," he says. "You can move in as soon as you're discharged from the hospital."

"That's brilliant, thank you," I smile.

"You don't look overly happy about it," Aidan says frowning.

"Oh no it's not that. I am happy about it," I say quickly. "It's just … well I feel a little bit bad about it only being temporary. I don't want to leave your sister in the lurch when it's time for me to go home."

Aidan shakes his head.

"You won't. I've told her it'll only be for a few weeks. And it's not like she's actively looking for someone to rent the room and you're taking it up when she could get someone long term in there."

"Then consider it sold," I smile. "Seriously. Thank you for this. Do I need to get a deposit to her?"

"Your rent will be one hundred dollars a week. That includes all of your utilities so there will just be food to buy. Nadia, that's my sister, said not to worry about any of this while you're still in hospital. The two of you can sort it out once you're discharged," Aidan says.

"Thanks," I smile again.

The door to my room opens and Stacy walks in.

"Aidan we have to stop meeting like this," she purrs, grinning at him.

He returns her smile with a polite one of his own. Stacy looks momentarily hurt but she recovers herself quickly and turns to me.

"Time for your vitals," she says.

She moves towards me with the trolley and begins to attach the blood pressure cuff to me. She is barely focused on what she's doing. She can't keep her eyes off Aidan for more than a second or two. I probably should be annoyed about that, but I know where Stacy is coming from. I can barely keep my eyes off Aidan for more than two seconds either.

"Can you hand me the patient's chart please?" Stacy says to Aidan.

He reaches down and gets it and holds it out to her. She makes a point of touching his fingers with hers as she takes it. She smiles, trying to hold Aiden's gaze, but he has already looked away from her, his eyes back on me.

"So that's all sorted then," he says.

"Yes," I agree. "Thank you again."

"What's sorted?" Stacy asks.

"Erika is going to be renting a room from my sister for a while. You know, in case her attacker comes back," Aidan says.

"Oh, sorry to be so nosey," Stacy says, looking anything but sorry. "I thought it was a medical thing."

"If it was, it would have been in her chart," Aidan points out.

"Yeah, I guess it would," Stacy says, acting embarrassed. She turns her attention to me with what seems like a lot of effort and jots down my vitals. "You know it's pretty unlikely your attacker will come back."

"I know I'm just being paranoid but ..." I start.

"You're not being paranoid, you're being sensible," Aidan cuts in. "And all of these people telling you that you'll probably be ok aren't the ones to risk going back there and seeing if that's true or not."

"Aww, would you listen to that. Your knight in shining armour," Stacy laughs.

She nudges Aidan with her shoulder. He smiles at her; a smile I don't think is entirely real. That could just be wishful thinking though. I mean its clear Stacy likes Aidan as more than just a colleague. And she is gorgeous. Tall and slim and with a pretty face. There's no way Aidan could say she wasn't attractive. Maybe Aidan is into Stacy and he's just being nice to me; going the extra mile for a patient and all that.

I don't really know how I feel about that. I shouldn't care one way or the other really. I only met Aidan yesterday and it's not like I could say I know him. He's been by my room a fair few times – more than I think is normal for a doctor to drop in on a patient who isn't particularly sick – but does that really mean everything I want it to mean? And that there is my answer. That's why I care. Because whether Aidan is into me or not, I want him to be. Because I am very much into him.

As much as I hate to admit it, I'm jealous of Stacy. I know it's irrational and stupid, but it's there all the same.

"All done," Stacy smiles at me. She turns to Aidan. "Any idea when Ms Hart will be able to go to her apartment then?"

Is it possible Stacy is jealous of me too and that she wants me out of the way? No, I tell myself. She's just doing her job. Asking as a nurse so she knows when the bed will be free for the next patient no doubt.

"If everything stays as good as it is looking, then I see no reason why you'll be here for much longer Erika," Aidan says. He glances at Stacy. "Of course with the amnesia we do have to be a little bit more careful, so perhaps another two or three days."

A idan was true to his word. My vitals all stayed good and two days have passed and I'm finally being discharged from the hospital. I just have to wait for my painkillers to be delivered and then I'm free to go. I'll miss Aidan's daily visits, sometimes two or three a shift but I will be glad to get out of this place. Like really glad. Don't get me wrong, it's a good thing that we have hospitals and I understand that if you're ill, they're likely the best place to be. But I wasn't ill and my stay was more precautionary than anything. I have been so bored I could tear my hair out.

My only reprieve from the boredom was my visit from Jennifer and of course the daily visits from Aidan. I think his visits kept me sane. They certainly gave me something to look forward to. It got to the point where we were openly flirting with each other, and when Aidan wasn't in my room, I found myself fantasizing about him and about what it would be like to be in his arms, to be kissed by him, fucked by him.

Finally, after waiting a good few hours after being told I was discharged, Aidan appears in my room again. He holds up a little white box and smiles at me.

"Your meds," he says. "Has anyone been over the instructions for taking them with you?"

I nod my head.

"Yeah. Take two of them four times a day with water for the next week," I say.

"You're a fast learner," Aidan grins at me.

"I had a good teacher," I smile back.

"Look I know you probably can't wait to see the back of this place, but with your head injury, we're not really meant to discharge patients unless there's someone with them. I mean you can obviously call someone to come and get you, or if you don't mind waiting a little longer, my shift ends in an hour. I can take you to Nadia's place and introduce the two of you," Aidan says.

I debate it for a moment, but there's really no question about what I want to do. Not only will arriving at Nadia's place with Aidan be a lot less awkward, but I really want to have the chance to spend some time with him outside of the hospital, and I'm afraid that if I say no to this, Aidan will take it as me saying no to anything happening between us in the future.

"I'll wait," I say.

Aidan smiles. A warm, happy smile that tells me I gave him the right answer about waiting for him.

AIDAN

I walk along the corridor towards Erika's room, my white coat left behind in my office. I am just a civilian now to anyone passing me by. No one but the other staff here would know I was a doctor now. I'm just wearing jeans, a t-shirt and a black jacket.

I so badly want to get to Erika's room and get her out of here before either an emergency arises that I need to deal with before I can leave, or someone spots me and Erika leaving together and makes a big deal out of it. I confess I like Erika. I really do. And I really want to see more of her once she's out of the hospital. And technically she's signed the discharge papers and is no longer my patient, but I still think it would be wise to at least wait until after she's officially left the place to have colleagues whispering about us.

I don't know what it is about Erika that got my attention so quickly and then never let it go, but the way I feel when I look at her is like nothing I've ever felt before. I mean obviously she's hot and when I look at her, I want to taste her lips, taste her pussy, make love to her all night long. I want to hold her in my arms and never let her go. But it's more than that.

There is something vulnerable about Erika, and whenever I look at her, I just get this overwhelming urge to protect her. In my line of work, I see a lot of people who have been hurt by others, and while I'm always angry on their behalf, I have never felt it so strongly as I do with Erika. And I have certainly never called my sister and persuaded her to let a patient move in with her before.

It doesn't help that the police are no closer to finding Erika's attacker than they were when they brought her in to the hospital. The DNA sample they found didn't match their records and neither did any of the fingerprints. The CCTV angle didn't pan out – it seems like there are no active cameras close enough to Erika's place to show anyone going to or from her property with any certainty. Her elderly neighbour who called the police hadn't seen anything, and all he could say for sure was a male voice shouted something he couldn't make out and there was a lot of banging. That didn't give the police much to go on as they had already ascertained the attacker was likely a male by the size of the hand prints on Erika's neck. None of her other neighbours had seen or heard anything suspicious or out of the ordinary. It was all just a bunch of dead ends.

Officially the investigation is still open and the officers claim they're still actively working the case, but I have my doubts about whether or not that's true. I don't doubt the case is still open – they have to leave it open if it's not solved – but I seriously doubt they're spending anymore man hours on it.

I'm so glad Erika agreed to take the room at Nadia's place. The thought of her being back in her own place alone so soon after the attack fills me with worry. I'm sure the police are right. That everyone is right. That the attacker is unlikely to come back. But that doesn't mean it's impossible and I'll just feel better knowing Erika is safely away from her house. And if I'm being honest, I like the idea of being able to drop around and see her without looking like a creep.

Dropping around to see Erika at home could be seen as me crossing a major line and Erika could well be forgiven for thinking I was being creepy. But dropping round to see my sister whenever I want to isn't weird and if that gives Erika and I a chance to get know each other a little better, then that can only be a good thing.

I reach Erika's room and tap on the door. I push it open when she calls for me to come in. She looks gorgeous. She's wearing a pair of jeans and a white blouse with the top two buttons open, giving me just a hint of cleavage. She is sitting on the chair beside her bed with her bag in her lap. When she sees me, she smiles and her eyes twinkle.

"Are you ready?" I ask. She's already getting to her feet before I even finish the question and I laugh. "I'll take that as a yes then."

"Oh God you have no idea. I am so ready to get out of here," Erika says, moving past me through the door I'm holding open. We head for the exit.

I can't help but wonder if she means to get away from me, but I dismiss that as stupid. She just means she's glad to get out of the hospital and of course she is. Who wants to be stuck in hospital once they're feeling better? It's bad enough being stuck in there when you're feeling ill.

As though she can read my mind, she flashes me a quick sideways look and smiles at me.

"I'll miss our little chats though. It was nice having you keep dropping by my room."

"I can still drop by and see you while you're at Nadia's," I point out.

She smiles again, a teasing flirty smile this time.

"Whatever will your sister think if you come and visit me in my room?"

"That's not exactly what I meant," I say quickly, afraid I've upset her.

"Shame," she grins.

I don't quite know what to say to that so I go with the safest option; saying nothing. We've almost reached my car so I'm saved from an awkward silence when I point to my car and tell Erika it's that one. She veers off towards it. I take her bag and put it in the trunk and then we get into the car. I thought about going around and opening Erika's door for her, but she was already in the car before I decided whether it would be too much or not. She doesn't seem annoyed that I didn't open the door for her.

"So where's your sister's place then?" Erika asks as I fire up the car engine and start to pull out of my parking space.

"It's not far from here actually. It's over on the west side of town," I say.

"Oh that's only a couple of blocks from my place. That's good because if I stay a while, it means work will still be easy enough to get to," Erika says.

"Where do you work?" I ask her.

Now we're off the hospital property and out of the grounds, I am officially not Erika's doctor anymore and that means it's ok to ask her personal questions not related to her medical history or anything. It also means its ok to date her. It still feels kind of like crossing a line dating an ex-patient, but if Erika agreed to date me, I wouldn't care about that. I mean it's not like she came in for anything intimate or that I learned anything weird or personal about her during her stay.

"At the North Fell Nursery. I'm a nursery nurse," Erika says.

"No wonder you didn't complain about your head," I grin. "You must have an almost permanent headache."

"You get used to it," Erika says.

"The headache?"

"No." She laughs and puts her hand on my thigh for a second as she does it. I feel my cock responding to her touch almost instantly and I'm glad my t-shirt and jacket are covering my crotch. "The constant noise and activity. You get used to that. It even becomes kind of strange not being surrounded by it all on your day off. I miss it now and to be honest, the only reason I really agreed to having a few weeks on sick pay is because the bruises around my neck would scare half of the kids."

"You don't want to rush back to work Erika. Even aside from the bruises. You have suffered a trauma that was bad enough for your mind to block out the memories of it. That's not something to make light of."

"I know what you mean, but it's funny. Because I can't remember the attack, I guess it's also easy to forget how serious it could have been if that makes sense," Erika says.

"It does. And that's often why your subconscious blanks the memory out so that you're not constantly reliving it and making yourself ill with worry," I say. "But don't be fooled into thinking that means you can go off and run a marathon tomorrow."

Erika laughs softly.

"Shame. That was exactly what I was going to do tomorrow as well," she says.

I shake my head but I'm laughing. I pull onto Nadia's street and park my car out in front of her building.

"Here we are," I say.

Erika

I smile as I look at the building we have pulled up outside of. It's a nice building, in a nice, quiet area of town. It looks clean and welcoming and that's a relief. I also can't help but feel instantly safer just for knowing that there's an intercom system so no one can get into the building without permission. This is good because it means that random people looking to cause trouble are unlikely to target the building knowing they can't just knock on a door and then force their way inside.

We get out of the car and head to the door. Aidan presses the buzzer for apartment number seventeen. That's another good thing. The apartment is listed as being on the third floor. I like the idea of not being low enough for someone to break a window out and get inside of the apartment that way. Although I have just told Aidan that I forget how serious the attack could have been, and that's true, I am also aware that the attack has made me more conscious of home security, maybe even to the point of paranoia.

A female voice greets us through the intercom and I forget my worries for a moment and focus on that.

"It's us," Aidan says.

"Come on up," the voice replies.

There's a buzzing sound and Aidan pulls the door. He holds it open and I step into the building. It smells of disinfectant and cooking smells. That's good. It feels both clean and homely. Aidan follows me into the building and leads me to the elevator. He presses the button for the third floor and we ride up in the surprisingly quick elevator. We come out in a carpeted hallway and Aidan turns to the right. I follow him. Apartment seventeen is the second door down from the elevator. Aidan knocks on it and it's pulled open in seconds.

A woman smiles as she stands back and lets us in. She looks a couple of years younger than Aidan, probably about my age. She has long dark brown hair which she's wearing half up and half down. She's wearing neon blue leggings, sneakers and a white crop top. Her figure is stunning.

"You must be Erika," she smiles warmly.

I nod my head and extend my hand. Nadia ignores my outstretched hand and pulls me into a hug.

"I'm Nadia," she says. "And whatever my brother here has told you about me is lies."

"Well, all he's really told me is that your name is Nadia and you wanted a roommate but didn't like the idea of advertising for one," I tell her.

"Ok, strangely, that's not lies," she laughs. She steps back and gestures down to her clothes. "Excuse the outfit. I have my yoga class soon. Don't worry though, I'll have time to show you around first. Aidan? Why don't you start the coffeemaker?"

Aidan gives her an amused look and then he heads off to do what she asked, going through a door off the hallway. Nadia points to the door Aidan has just disappeared through. He has closed the door behind him so I don't get to see a glimpse of the kitchen. It's a shame because the kitchen is usually my favorite room in any house, but I'm sure I'll see it soon enough.

"So obviously that's the kitchen and dining area," Nadia says. She nods to another door. "Through here is the living room."

She walks away and I follow her into the living room. It's fairly big and it's decorated nicely in understated creams and terracotta colours. She leads me through the living room and down another short hallway.

"The door at the end is the bathroom," she tells me. "The one on the right is my room. And this one is your room."

She opens the door and I step inside to take a look. It's a small room, just big enough for a double bed, a dresser and a chest of drawers and pretty much nothing else, but it's not like I need anything else. It's only a temporary arrangement, and really the only difference between this room and my room at home is I have a nightstand at home. I guess I'll just have to live with no reading lamp and get up to turn the light off after reading in bed.

The walls are a pale lilac colour. The curtains, carpet and bedding are a darker shade of purple. A white lightshade matches the white paintwork. I move to the window and look out. I find myself looking down into a good sized outdoors area with a small pool surrounded by sun loungers and plenty of grass and flower beds.

"We can use this area?" I ask.

Nadia nods and smiles.

"Yes. Although I have to warn you the pool is by far the coldest pool I've ever been in."

I wince and she laughs.

"Yeah exactly," she says. "The coffee should be ready by now. Let's go through to the living room and sit for five minutes before I have to go and then you can get yourself settled in."

She's already walking away towards the living room as she says it and I follow her. Aidan is sitting on the couch, his legs crossed. He holds a steaming mug of coffee and two more sit on the table. Nadia picks one up and takes the chair leaving me to share the couch with Aidan. I can't say that is a bad thing. I sit down and sip my coffee as Nadia goes over the building rules and the rent payments and everything. I like her. She's to the point and she seems nice, like someone I would be friends with.

At the end of the conversation, she hands me a key on a little blue heart keyring. I thank her and push it into my pocket. Nadia checks her watch and jumps up.

"Well I have to go. Get settled in Erika, make yourself at home. I'll only be about an hour or so and then maybe we can have dinner together and get to know each other a little bit better?"

"That would be nice," I smile. "It won't take me long to unpack. I've only … dammit."

"What is it?" Nadia asks frowning.

"My bag. I left it in the car."

I start to stand up, but Aidan jumps up and waves me back down.

"It's ok, I'll go," he says.

I smile my thanks at him.

"I'll get Nadia to let me back in so you don't have to buzz me up," he adds.

I watch them leave and then I go to look at the kitchen. It's much bigger than I was expecting it to be and the little dining table for two I was expecting is actually a huge wooden thing with six chairs fitted comfortably around it. The kitchen itself has a large stove, a microwave and a massive refrigerator freezer. I am going to be in my element here. I have always enjoyed cooking and I love the freedom of a big kitchen so I can move around easily.

I leave the kitchen behind and cut back through the living room and go to check out the bathroom. It's basic but functional with a bath/shower combination, a sink and a toilet. It's all covered with shining white tiles and I am pleased that everything is clean and neat. Nadia and I are going to get on just fine. I don't think I could live with a slob, not even for a little while.

For half a second, I debate looking into Nadia's room but I decide against it. Talk about a good way to piss off your host before you're even unpacked. Instead, I go back into my room and look out of the window again. I hear the front door open as I look down at the garden area.

"I'm through here," I call out.

For an awful second, panic grips me as the footsteps come closer to me. What if my attacker followed me and found me here? I tell myself to get a grip and I am back under control when the door opens and Aidan appears with my bag.

"Thanks." I say. "For getting my bag and for getting me this place."

"Anytime," Aidan smiled as he holds my bag out to me.

I take the bag, feeling his fingers brushing against mine and in that moment, I want nothing more than to throw the bag aside and pull Aidan against me and kiss him. And then push him back onto the bed and climb on top of him and make love to him. I can feel my face flushing at my thoughts, but I force myself to keep my eyes on Aidan's eyes without letting embarrassment turn me away from him. His eyes seem to hold mine in place and after a moment, I become aware that we are both panting slightly as we stand looking into each other's eyes, the air around us strangely charged.

Aidan looks away, looking flustered suddenly.

"I should get going then," he says.

He turns and heads for the door and I can't think of what I can say to stop him. I don't want him to leave, and certainly not like this. His hand is on the door handle when suddenly, he turns back to me. He closes the gap between us in two strides and pushes his hands into my hair, his lips finding mine.

I'm a little shocked at first, but I soon recover and I melt into Aidan's kiss, my body responding to him instantly, my pussy wet and my nipples hard. I move closer to Aidan until I am pressed up against his body. I wrap my arms around him, kissing him deeper.

His kiss is every bit as amazing as I thought it would be. He tastes of sweet coffee and cinnamon and his lips move perfectly in sync with mine as if they have just been waiting to meet. He moves his hands from my hair, running his fingers gently over my face and then he moves his hands down over my ribs and rests them on my hips. His touch spreads liquid fire through me and I shiver as he moves his hands again, cupping my ass and pulling me tighter against him.

He starts to walk me backwards and I let myself be moved. My hands push underneath his t-shirt, running over the smooth muscular skin on his back. His hands move back to my hips again and he pushes me against the wall. He moves his lips from mine, kissing over my chin and then he starts to kiss down my neck. his touch there is painful and despite me trying to keep it in, a gasp escapes my lips and Aidan looks up at me in time to catch my grimace of pain.

He jumps back from me as if I am suddenly burning him.

"Shit. Erika I'm sorry. You've just been assaulted and here I am throwing myself at you, and ... I should go."

He starts to move towards the door again, but this time, I do stop him. I step forward and grab his wrist.

"Aidan wait," I say.

He looks back at me, the pain and embarrassment on his face clear to see. I lead him to the bed and sit down on the edge of it, patting the spot beside me. Aidan hesitates for a moment, but then he sits down beside me where I touched. I can feel his thigh touching mine and I know I am right to sit him down and talk to him now. I can't lose him because of one stupid, awkward moment.

"I'm sorry I flinched. I really didn't mean to," I start.

"You have nothing to apologize for. I'm the one who hurt you," Aidan says.

"But it was an accident. I know it was. And I don't want you to go running off before I tell you this." I pause and look at Aidan, waiting until he looks back at me before I go on. "I want you Aidan."

Aidan swallows hard. I see his Adam's apple move in his throat. He looks a little taken aback by what I've said but he's smiling.

"I want you too," he says. "Like I've never wanted anyone. But not yet. Not until you're feeling better."

I nod my head. I want him now. I don't care if it hurts my neck, I would put up with the pain to have him, but I know that's an argument I'm not going to win. He leans in and kisses me on the lips, a soft kiss this time. His lips linger on mine for a moment and then he gets up.

"I really should go though. It wouldn't look too good if Nadia comes home and catches me in your bedroom on your first day at her place would it?" Aidan laughs.

I laugh and shake my head.

"No. It's not exactly the impression I want to make on her," I agree.

I stand up and walk Aidan to the door. He kisses me again in the open doorway.

"I'll stop by some time tomorrow and see how you're doing," he says. He digs in his pocket and hands me a card. "In the meantime, here's my number. Call me anytime if you don't feel right. Or just, you know, because you want to."

I pull my phone out of my own pocket and quickly enter his number in it. I hit call and his phone rings in his pocket.

"And now you have my number. Call me whenever you want, but I have to say, if you don't feel right, you're probably best off calling someone else," I say. "You know, like one of the hundreds of actual doctors or nurses you know."

Aidan laughs and kisses me again and then he's walking down the corridor.

"I know you're watching my ass," he calls over his shoulder.

"Busted," I giggle.

I close the door, still laughing. I go back to my room to unpack my tiny bag and it's clear to me almost immediately that tomorrow, I'm going to have to pop back to my place and collect some more of my stuff. I need more clothes of course, but it's other stuff too like towels and bedding, cutlery and pans. I can't just expect to keep using Nadia's things.

I unpack quickly – I don't have enough stuff with me for it to take long – and then I wander back through to the living room. I debate starting to make some dinner for Nadia and me. It was her idea for me to have dinner with her, so I don't think she'll mind me using some of her food. I decide against it. It feels too forward. I have no idea what she likes to eat or how she likes stuff cooked. I'll wait for her to get home and then offer to cook.

ERIKA

Nadia came back home not long after I had finished unpacking my few things. I was lying on the couch watching the TV when I heard the front door open and Nadia shouted hello. I almost jumped into a sitting position but I reminded myself if I was going to be living here now that I was allowed to sit comfortably.

I had offered to cook dinner for us, but Nadia insisted on calling for pizza, saying it was her treat. By the time she had showered and changed, the pizzas had arrived. We ate them at the dining room table discussing my rent and the house rules. Nadia seemed pretty chilled out and the rules she had were the sort of rules I would have had too if the roles were reversed. They were common sense rules like who would clean what and when and how we would go about having house guests. We organized a schedule for the cleaning in the apartment and agreed that guests where fine. We also agreed there and then that if either of us had a problem with the other one, we would speak about it immediately instead of letting it fester out of control. The more we talked and established how this was going to work, the more I liked Nadia's straight forward approach to things.

After our rule talk, we moved on to more general things and I told Nadia I planned on going home the next day to collect some of my stuff. She waved away my idea of bringing bedding and towels and kitchen supplies telling me there was plenty of everything and whatever I could find I was welcome to use. We agreed that Nadia would continue doing the weekly shopping for things we would both use like bread, milk and toilet paper, that kind of thing, and that I would give her half of the money and then we'd buy our own favorite and preferred food.

After we had eaten the pizza, Nadia grabbed two beers from the fridge and handed me one. We went through to the living room and sat drinking them. We are onto our third bottle now.

"Aidan said you'd just graduated from college," I say. "What did you study? Medicine?"

"God no," Nadia laughed. "Let Aidan deal with the vomit and the blood and who knows what else. I did a marketing degree. I worked for a few years as a marketing assistant before I went to college and I felt like I had so many ideas to offer, but no one took me seriously without the degree. One day I got sick of it and went and got the degree."

"So you're going back to your old firm?" I ask.

"No way. They didn't want me when they had me. I'm starting at a new firm in a few weeks."

"Sounds good," I say. "I thought maybe you were one of those families where you all went down the medical route."

"Not at all," Nadia said shaking her head. "Aidan is the first one in our family to go down that route. Our dad is a lawyer and our mom is an office manager. I know it sounds like a cliché, but Aidan genuinely wanted to help people and so he got into medicine."

"That's a good reason to do it," I say. "And he really does help people. I mean he found me a place to live and everything. He must really care about his patients."

Nadia laughs and I frown at her. She shakes her head but she's still laughing a little.

"Look I'm not saying Aidan isn't a good doctor because he is, but if you think he goes that far for each of his patients then you're crazy," Nadia said.

"I don't understand," I say.

"He likes you Erika. You must have noticed," Nadia says.

I look down into my lap and nod my head, my cheeks flushing slightly. I would blame the beer but it's a little too obvious they only reddened at the mention of Aidan liking me for that to wash and so I don't say anything about it.

"Do you feel the same way about him?" Nadia asks.

I nod again.

"Thank God for that," Nadia says. "Because I haven't seen him like this in years."

"What do you mean?" I ask, finally daring to look up from my lap.

"Aidan has been a workaholic since his first day as an intern at the hospital. He's worked his way up, but his work ethic has never changed. Work, work and more work. That was Aidan's life. He didn't date because the job was more important to him than actually having a life. But I saw the way he looked at you earlier Erika. He's really into you," Nadia says.

I can't help but smile at her words, because I am really into Aidan too and to hear that even his own sister thinks he feels the same way about me has pretty much made my night.

"That's mostly why I agreed to you having the room," Nadia goes on. "I mean it was true that I was worried about getting stuck with a weirdo and Aidan is a pretty good judge of character so I figured I was probably safe from that if I went on his recommendation. But when he spoke about you, there was something in his voice that told me he thought you were special and that he wanted you in his life."

I smile again. I can't seem to stop smiling. The more Nadia reveals, the more it sounds like Aidan really is into me. It proves that his kiss wasn't just a spur of the moment thing that he might end up regretting. He actually likes me. It makes me even more glad that I told him I wanted him and it takes away the worry that he only agreed that he wanted me too in case he hurt my feelings.

"I hope I haven't said too much," Nadia says suddenly and I realise I haven't really spoken since she started telling me about Aidan. She probably thinks she's scaring me off or something.

"Not at all," I say quickly. I debate how much to tell her. I like Nadia and she doesn't sound like she'll be pissed off if she thinks I'm into her brother. I decide to tell her the truth. "I really like Aidan too. We kissed earlier. And we exchanged numbers."

Nadia beams at me and I know I made the right decision telling her about our kiss.

"So what about you? Do you have a boyfriend?" I ask.

Nadia shrugs and shakes her head.

"Not really. I mean there's Brent, but we're not really boyfriend and girlfriend. We're just casual," she says,

"Do you want it to be more?" I ask.

I know I'm being nosey but the beer is loosening my tongue enough that I just ask the question that's on my mind. Nadia can always tell me to mind my own business if she wants to.

"I don't know. Maybe. Some days I think I do and then other days I tell myself I like being single," Nadia says. "I mean I like Brent, but that's it. I'm not sure it will ever be more than that."

"It sounds like me and my ex to be honest. He was a nice guy but there was no spark between us and I called it off in the end," I say.

"Maybe that's what I should do," Nadia says. "Just cut Brent off and have a clean break. I think I would miss him if I did that though."

"Maybe wait a little longer and see how it goes then. Usually if you miss someone when you're not with them it means you're into them," I point out.

Nadia nods thoughtfully.

"Yeah you're probably right. And a few more weeks won't hurt will it?"

I shake my head and she leans across and clinks her bottle against mine.

"Cheers," she smiles. "I could get used to this roommate thing."

"Me too," I agree.

I was worried it would be awkward between Nadia and me but it's been far from it. I was also worried I wouldn't like having someone else in my living space after living alone for so long, but again, so far, it's far from that. It's nice having someone to have dinner with and talk about boys with.

I had planned on going by my house this morning and collecting some of my things, but when I was making some coffee, Nadia came in and asked me if I fancied a little bit of retail therapy. She told me she was going out for an early dinner with friends and then onto a little cocktail bar afterwards and she wanted a nice dress to wear. I decided it would be fun to spend the day with Nadia, even though I didn't want to blow money on clothes and shoes I didn't need. And then I told myself I could go over to the house once Nadia was out. It would fill in some time that I otherwise would just be spending alone. Recovering from the attack, being on sick leave and not having anything to do to fill my days was going to take some getting used to.

We went to the shopping center and tried on tons of outfits. We grabbed lunch in the food court and Nadia bought a beautiful red dress for her night out. She's gone now and I'm just putting my jacket on ready to go to my house.

I grab my keys and my phone and I set off walking. I stop in a small supermarket on the way and grab some food for dinner. When I leave the supermarket, I walk fast and I'm at my house in under fifteen minutes including the stop for groceries.

I stand in my small garden staring at the front door. I'm nervous, afraid to go inside almost. I am worried that being back in the house will trigger my memories and I'll have to relive the attack all over again. I tell myself that if that does happen, it will be a good thing. I can call Officer Prescott and tell her who the hell did this to me.

With that thought in mind, I fish my keys out of my pocket, unlock the front door, push it open slowly and step inside. The familiar smell hits me first. The jasmine air freshener that I like. The scent of my perfumes lingering in the air. The hallway is undisturbed and I walk down it on slightly shaky legs. I push the living room door open and I gasp when I see the room.

The coffee table is broken, its legs snapped. One of them has a rust coloured stain on the end of it and my hand unconsciously goes to the cut on my head when I see it. It's blood from my head. I force my eyes from the blood stain and keep looking around. My TV is on the ground, smashed. Shards of it lay all over. My picture from above the fire place is on the ground, torn. I feel tears coming into my eyes and I blink them away quickly.

I know I need to start cleaning up the mess but I can't face it just yet. I decide to go and pack my things first and take a look around to see if anything has been stolen like Officer Prescott asked me to do. The brief glance around the living room tells me nothing has been taken and I move through to

69

the kitchen. Nothing is even an inch out of place in here. I go upstairs and find much the same thing. A few things in my bathroom and bedroom look like they've been moved, but nothing has been taken and I think the things that have been moved must be due to Jennifer getting my things together for me.

I grab a large wheeled suitcase and open it on my bed. I go to my closet and start packing my clothes. I move on to my chest of drawers and it's not too long until pretty much all of my clothes are in the suitcase except my work clothes. I'll come back for them when I get to go back to work.

I grab a smaller suitcase from the bottom of the wardrobe and fill it with the rest of my toiletries, make up and hair products. I wheel the two suitcases down the hallway and drag them down the stairs to the front door. I go back to the living room. It doesn't feel like quite such a shock to the system this time as I'm expecting the mess and chaos.

I go to the kitchen and grab a sweeping brush and a dust pan and a roll of black sacks. I go back to the living room and begin to tackle the mess. I have made a good start on it when I hear a knocking at my front door. My heart instantly starts to race and sweat bursts out on the palms of my hands, the soles of my feet and my scalp. I tell myself to calm down. It's probably old Mr Pritchard from next door wanting to see if I'm ok. That reminds me. I really should go and thank him for calling the police the night of my attack.

Cautiously, aware of the shards still on the ground around me, I push myself up from my knees. I move towards the door, trying to keep calm. The chances of my attacker coming back the very moment I happen to have come back has got to be too much of a coincidence to actually be happening.

"Who is it?" I call as I reach the hallway, not liking the way my voice sounds at all. It sounds shaky and nervous.

"It's Jeremy."

Oh great. That's all I need. I don't feel strong enough to fend him off right now.

"I'm not here to try to get you to change your mind about us Erika. I just want to make sure you're ok," he adds.

I sigh and open the door. What's the point of not opening it? He knows I'm here.

"Why wouldn't I be ok?" I ask when the door is open.

Jeremy gasps as his eyes go to my neck.

"I heard about the attack. Jeez Erika, look what they did to you," he says.

"I'm ok. Really. It looks worse than it is," I say.

Jeremy frowns in concern.

"Do the police have the guy who did this to you?" he asks.

I shake my head.

"No. I can't remember anything about the attack so they don't really have anything to go on," I tell him.

"But your memory will come back right?" he says.

I shrug.

"It could , but there's a chance it won't," I say.

"Is being here alone a good idea?" Jeremy asks me.

"I'm staying with a friend for now," I tell him. I don't want to get into the fact that I've only just met Nadia and I certainly don't want to get into how I met her. "I just dropped by to collect some of my things. And then I started trying to sort out the mess. The attacker trashed the living room."

"Bastard," Jeremy says, shaking his head. "What sort of a monster does shit like this?"

I just shake my head, unsure of what I'm meant to say to him.

"Let me come in and help you clean up," Jeremy says.

"You don't have to do that," I say.

"I know I don't have to," he smiles. "But I want to."

I hesitate and he smiles again.

"Look Erika I know I was a bit crazy for a few days after we broke up, but I swear I'm not going to try anything. I've accepted that it's over between us, but I would like us still to be friends. And what sort of a friend would I be if I walked away now and didn't help you?"

He sounds genuine enough and to be honest, I could use some help. I'll never get the body of the TV outside to my bin on my own and I will feel a whole lot less creeped out being back here if I have someone with me.

"Well if you're sure …" I say.

"I am," Jeremy insists and I stand back and let him inside.

JEREMY

I can't believe Erika was gullible enough to let me into her home again. I suppose that's not fair. She was gullible the first time. This time though, she genuinely doesn't know any better. I can't believe this worked out so well for me to be honest. It feels like it might be too good to be true.

I came here this evening to find out exactly how much Erika knew about what had happened to her. I heard about the attack from one of her friends I ran into in a café yesterday. Or should I say I heard about why the police hadn't already been to my door from one of Erika's friends in a café yesterday. Her friend told me all about her little bout of amnesia, and while I had no reason to doubt her friend, I wanted to hear it myself directly from Erika. And I was curious to know if her doctors thought her memory would come back any time soon. Coming here was a risky move, but I had to know or I knew I would drive myself crazy thinking about it.

From what she's said so far, I'm pretty much in the clear. I should call it my lucky day and get the hell out of here and never see Erika again. But here's the thing. I meant it when I said that if I can't have her then no one else can have her either. I almost fucked up everything between us, but I have been given a second chance. A second chance to make Erika mine. And I intend to keep it and get my girl back.

Last time I came here things didn't go well. It all escalated so quickly, but I didn't come to her place with the intention to hurt Erika. I intended to show her all of the reasons we were good together. But then she started acting like she thought she was better than me and I got angry and I hurt her. This time, I will keep my temper. I have sworn it to myself.

I will keep sweeping up the mess in Erika's place with her and act all concerned and friendly and like I'm worried about her, and I'll make her see that I am someone she wants around. And let's face it, it'll help that she thinks she needs protecting in case whoever did this to her comes back again. Oh the irony of that.

It's pissing me off a bit that I made such a fucking mess here. If I had known I'd end up being here for the clean up, I might have taken it a bit easier. Especially on the damned TV. There are parts of that thing every fucking where.

"Jeremy?" Erika says in her sweet little voice. I glance up and she's smiling at me. That smile she always used to give me when she wanted something. "I know this is really presumptuous, but can I ask another favour?"

"It's not presumptuous. You can ask me for anything," I say.

And I will give it to you to prove that you need me, I don't add.

"Will you help me take the bulk of the TV and the cabinet and the broken up table down to the dumpster please?"

"Sure," I smile. I grab the largest piece of the TV in one hand and two table legs in the other. "Lead the way."

I can't help but wonder if it's all worth it at this point. I mean this is a lot of work for a girl who broke up with me. I tell myself it's worth it. She's worth it. This is all just a part of our love story. We can tell our grandkids all about it all – how grandma was stupid and didn't know what was good for her, so grandad had to show her, and then they all lived happily ever after.

I reach the end of the hallway and Erika squeezes between me and the wall so she can open the door. She has the other two table legs and the smashed up canvas in her hand. That's it. She's letting me do the thick of the carrying, taking advantage of my good nature.

I can feel myself getting angry again and it must show on my face, because when Erika has unlocked the door, she turns to me to say something and instead, she frowns when she looks at me. I have to keep a grip on my emotions until I get her back. It's the only way. I can't risk triggering her memory and having her remember the attack.

She steps outside and I follow her around to the side of the house, towards the back yard and the dumpster.

"What's wrong?" I ask her as she glances at me again, as though she's the one acting weird.

"Nothing, I … Are you sure you're alright to help me Jeremy? Just you look kind of angry about it," she says.

An idea comes to me and I almost smile but I don't. That would ruin what I'm about to say completely.

"I'm not angry at you Erika. Or about helping you. Just seeing all of your things broken like this. That makes me angry. Like really angry. Who would do something like this?" I say.

Erika's face softens and she nods her head.

"I was angry too at first," she says. "Now I think I'm just trying to look on the positive side. I got out alive and I am trying to be thankful for that."

"I'm definitely thankful for that too," I say.

We've reached the dumpster. Erika opens it and deposits her few bits into it. I haul my things in and then I crush everything down so we can fit some more in. I turn back to Erika who smiles at me and quickly squeezes my arm.

"Thank you. For being mad on my behalf," she says.

I flash her a quick smile, not trusting myself with words right now. I am elated, my heart is singing. She squeezed my arm. She made an excuse to touch me. My plan is working. Erika is starting to see that she made a mistake letting me go. It's only a matter of time until she is mine once more now.

After Erika's touch on my arm, I'm no longer pissed off that I'm only meant to be helping her and yet somehow seem to be doing the bulk of the heavy lifting. In fact, I tell her I can take the rest out and she should stay in here. She argues at first, but it's the sort of argument someone puts up when they really want to lose. It's nothing like the way she would argue with me when I told her we were meant to be together and she disagreed. No she meant that one.

I brooded on it the whole way back to the dumpster. I had to break up the pieces of the coffee table a little bit more to get them to fit into the bin. It felt good smashing that lump of wood into bits. It got some of my anger out and I reminded myself once more that the past didn't matter now. I just had to look to the future. A future where Erika and I could be together again. She was starting to want that. She had touched my arm. I just have to keep it together and see it through until she's mine once more.

As I calm down, picturing Erika and me cuddled up on the couch together, I become aware of eyes on me. I glance up to see an old man peering over the fence watching me.

Great. The nosy neighbor strikes again.

Erika's house is a semi detached house and I have a feeling it was this nosy old bastard that called the cops the last time I was here. It had to be him. He was the only one who might have heard the banging and the shouting.

I am momentarily consumed by anger again but I swallow it down. Yelling at the old man isn't going to win me any points with Erika. And the more I think about it, the more I see that his calling the cops when he did was actually a good thing really. He stopped me before I could hurt Erika anymore. He gave me a chance to get her back. I can't help but be annoyed at him for interfering though. Another thought strikes me as I look at him. What if he saw me here that evening? What if he recognizes me?

I smile at him and he smiles back. It's a tentative smile, but it's a smile all the same. That's good. If he recognized me, I don't think he'd be smiling at all. No, he'd be back in his own house, calling the cops again. Interfering in things that don't concern him again.

He's still just standing there staring at me and I am standing staring back. I am aware this isn't normal behavior, not from either of us, and I force myself to act normally, like I would if I wasn't on edge and this happened.

"I'm sorry about all of this. Did the noise disturb you?" I ask.

Translation – Did the noise mean you simply had to come out and put your nose into my business once again?

"Not so much disturbed me," the old man says. "I was just worried when I heard so much banging. After what happened here last week."

"I'm Jeremy," I say with a smile. I walk towards the fence and offer the old man my hand. He shakes it, although he makes no effort to give me his name. "I'm a friend of Erika's. I'm helping her clean up the mess the attacker left. The noise you heard was me breaking up the coffee table so it would fit in the dumpster. The attacker broke it, but not enough for it just to drop in."

"Jeremy? Is everything ok?" Erika calls from behind me. "You've been out here for ages."

"Everything's fine," I call back. "I'm sorry to worry you. I was just talking to your neighbor."

The old man has relaxed now that Erika has called my name and made it clear she does indeed know me. His smile looks real this time.

"I'm sorry to have disturbed you," he says.

"Not at all," I say. "I'm just pleased Erika has a neighbor who looks out for her."

"I do what I can," the old man says with a proud smile.

"Mr Pritchard," Erika says warmly as she comes to stand beside me. "I was going to come and see you when I was finished cleaning up all of the mess inside. I wanted to thank you for calling the police. I assume it was you?" She pauses and Mr Pritchard nods. "You probably saved my life so thank you. And if there's ever anything I can do for you …"

Mr Pritchard waves her offer away.

"I just did what anyone would have done dear. I'm honestly just glad that you're ok. I wish I was twenty years younger and I would have come in and gotten rid of the bastard myself. What sort of a coward attacks a woman?"

I nod my head, agreeing with Mr Pritchard, but really, what does he know? It's not like I just decided to beat Erika up. She was making me angry, refusing to see sense, and it just kind of happened. And twenty years younger or not, if he had tried to stop me, he would have ended up regretting it.

"I would have been by sooner," Erika is saying. "But I've been staying with a friend. I just came by to get some things and I ended up sticking around to sort out some of the mess in the living room."

"Is it bad?" Mr Pritchard asks.

"It was pretty bad," Erika says. "But it's almost sorted now. Jeremy dropping in and giving me a hand really helped."

I beam at her. She's seeing it now. She's seeing that I can help her. That I can make her life easier.

"I'm glad you're ok anyway," Mr Pritchard says. "I'd best be getting back inside. Once you're back home, just knock on my door anytime if you need anything ok?"

"Thank you. And the same goes for you," Erika replies.

We stand in silence for a moment as Mr Pritchard heads away back to his house. Erika turns to me after a moment and smiles.

"He's such a nice man isn't he?" she says.

I nod my head. What else is there to do?

"He came over because he heard banging and wanted to see if everything was ok," I say when I realize the nod won't be enough.

"Banging?" Erika asks.

"I was breaking up the coffee table pieces to get them in the dumpster," I explain.

"Oh yeah. Of course," she says.

We head back to the house. While I've been out to the dumpster, Erika has finished the rest of the cleaning up and now the only thing out of place in the living room, except the obvious lack of furniture, is two black sacks full off trash.

"I'll take those out," I say, stepping towards them.

"Oh no it's fine. They're not that heavy. I'll just take them to the dumpster on my way out," she says.

"When were you planning on heading back to your friend's place?" I ask.

Erika looks uncomfortable for a moment, twisting her fingers together and looking down at the ground and I realize she wants to leave now and is waiting for me to leave so that she can, but she doesn't want to say so.

"It's ok if you want to say now," I tell her gently.

I would have liked for us to stay here for a while, just the two of us, but I don't want Erika to feel pressured. I want her to realize for herself that we're meant to be together and I want her to want to be with me because she wants to be, not because she feels like she has to be. Treating her gently like this will hopefully help her to see that for herself.

"I did kind of want to get going," she admits. "It gives me the creeps a little bit being here."

"Let's go then," I smile.

I place my hand on the small of her back and she doesn't shrug it away. I think this is starting to work, but I tell myself not to push it too far too fast. I don't want to scare Erika into pushing me away.

I start leading her towards the hall when she stops and turns back with a quiet gasp.

"The trash bags," she says, laughing and shaking her head. "I can't believe I forgot them so soon after we talked about them."

Was it because she was thinking about me? Because my hand on her back felt so good she couldn't think about anything else? Maybe. Hopefully.

Erika picks the bags up and comes back to where I wait for her just inside of the front door. I take the bags from her.

"I can carry them," she says.

"I know you can, but just because you can do something doesn't mean you have to," I smile.

She rolls her eyes but she smiles back at me. We reach the front door and she grabs her suitcases and lifts them through the door. I go off to the dumpster once more while she locks up the front door.

"Do you want this put out front?" I call out to her. "Only the trash men won't know it needs emptying if we leave it right back here."

"No its fine thanks," she calls back. "I'll sort it out once I move back home. It's not like its stuff that will spoil or anything."

I come back and take the large suitcase from Erika and hold out my hand for the small one.

"They're on wheels," she smiles. "I can manage them."

I don't argue with her. I don't want to argue with her ever again. But I keep the big suitcase. She extends the handle on the little one and I do the same on the big one and we walk down Erika's garden path. She pauses once we're out of the gate.

"Well thank you for stopping by and for helping me," she smiles. "I really do appreciate it."

"That sounds awfully like a goodbye," I say.

She just looks at me and I shake my head and smile at her.

"You don't honestly think I'm letting you walk to your friend's home on your own with two suitcases do you? Especially after what's just happened to you?" I say.

"I'm fine Jeremy. Seriously," she says.

I keep my tone of voice light, but I'm not backing down on this one. I want to know where this friend of hers lives in case I need to arrange to accidentally on purpose bump into Erika if she stops taking my calls again.

"Look, we've disturbed your neighbor once this evening with our banging. Do you really want to disturb him with the commotion of me throwing you over my shoulder and carrying you?" I say.

"Well when you put it that way, I guess you're walking me home then," Erika says with a soft laugh.

I smile along with her, happy to have won this one without having to resort to anything that could have been seen by Erika as going too far. Walking her home, keeping her safe, it all puts me in a good light, and it's all going to help to make Erika see her mistake in thinking we're not right for each other. And doing it all in a way that makes her laugh is a real bonus too.

Despite that, I feel a bit nervous. I don't like the idea of Erika living with someone else. It's going to make me getting access to her a little bit harder. If I want to see her, and drop around unannounced and Erika doesn't want to see me, she can just tell her roommate to say she's not home. I know when Erika and I are together, she's easy enough to persuade around to things, but when there's distance between us, she stands her ground easier. I think that's why she stopped responding to my texts and calls and cut me off on social media. I think she was starting to see she had made a mistake, but rather than risk seeing me and having to admit to it, she just stopped talking to me.

I can't let that happen again. I can't let our communications break down. I think the way to handle this now is to not try and get Erika to admit she made a mistake. I think the way to handle it is to just let her slowly come around to the idea of us again and just fall back into our routine and not discuss the time we spent apart. Just forget it ever happened.

I know what I have to do in regards to her roommate. I have to meet her and be utterly charming to her, get her to see what a good guy I am and how perfect Erika and I are together. If I can do that, she'll be less likely to play the gate keeper role for Erika and me. And she might even talk to Erika on my behalf (without me asking her to of course) about how we're right for each other and Erika should give me another chance. I decide that is my best course of action.

"So who is this friend you're living with?" I ask. "Anyone I know?"

Erika shakes her head.

"No. You two haven't met. Her name is Nadia."

"I figured you'd be staying with Jennifer. Or maybe Claudia," I say.

"There's no room at Jennifer's and she has more than enough on her plate right now," Erika says. "And Claudia is in Germany remember? She got that job over there."

"Oh of course. I forgot about that," I say.

It's a lie. I'm just curious as to why Erika is staying with some friend that wasn't even close enough for me to have met her. It comes to me quickly who this Nadia must be and I relax. She must be someone from the nursery Erika works at. The girls there are all pretty close but they don't really do the couples socializing thing so the only one from her work who I have met is Laura who we happened to run into on the street one afternoon. That must be it.

"How long until you can go back to work then?" I ask.

I know how much Erika loves her job and that she'll want to be getting back to it as quickly as possible.

"A couple of weeks," she says with a grimace. "I miss it already."

"Just concentrate on getting better for now," I say. "Work will still be there when you are feeling better."

"You sound like my doctor," Erika laughs.

"Then obviously your doctor is wise," I say, nudging her playfully with my elbow.

She rolls her eyes but she's laughing. I love her laugh. It's such a nice sound. So inviting and pretty. So … so Erika.

"Well this is me," Erika says after we've been walking for a couple more minutes.

She's stopped in front of an apartment block. I look around quickly. It's a nice enough area and I think she'll be safe here. The building itself looks well kept and although there is an intercom system, there's no door man and I think getting in would be easy enough. Usually in these set ups, if you ring every bell, someone will buzz you in without even bothering to answer the call. Or I could always say I was delivering something.

I shake the thoughts away. None of that is going to be necessary. Erika is coming around. She will buzz me in herself when I drop by, I know she will.

A few seconds have passed since Erika announced that this is her building and we're both just standing there, neither one of us speaking or moving. It's clear she has no intention of inviting me in right now, and this is getting awkward. Should I push for an invite or take it slower than that and just say goodbye and leave?

"It looks nice here," I say.

It's lame but it's something to break the silence while I decide how to play this.

"It is," Erika says, looking relieved at the break in the silence. I think her relief might also stem from me not asking if I can come in. That's not great, but it tells me that pushing her now might not be a good idea. "I think I'll settle in here well."

I decide that the best idea for me now might be to insist on helping Erika up the stairs with her suitcases. I won't ask to be invited in if she still doesn't extend the offer, but I think she will. It's much harder to turn someone away from your doorstep than it is to just not invite them into the building.

I open my mouth to tell her to lead the way when she smiles over my shoulder and waves. I glance behind me to see who is coming. Maybe this is my chance to start working on getting her roommate on our side.

It's not. The person Erika is smiling and waving at is a man. I feel rage burn inside of me, but I swallow it down quickly. Yes, the man is good looking. Yes, he looks like he works out. But that doesn't mean anything is happening with him and Erika. He could be a neighbor or anything.

He has reached us now and greeted Erika. Erika smiles warmly at him. This guy is no random neighbor. This is someone Erika has set her sights on. I can tell by the way she smiles at him, both warm and yet kind of coy at the same time. It's the way she used to smile at me.

I push the jealousy down once more. This guy was just a pit stop, someone Erika used to distract herself from thinking about me. But I'm back now, and he'll be out of the picture soon enough.

"Jeremy, this is Aidan, Nadia's brother," Erika says. "Aidan, this is my friend, Jeremy."

Friend huh? It'll be more than that soon enough. Hearing that this man is Nadia's brother would be reassuring to me if it wasn't for the way Erika looked at him when he first joined us and the way he's looking at her now. It would have explained who he was and why he was here. But now, looking at the way they are together, I think he's here for her. And getting him off the scene will be much harder when Erika is living with his sister. Dammit. This complicates things, but it'll all work out in the end. I'll make sure it does.

I force myself to smile at the enemy and extend my hand. Aidan shakes it. I wanted him to have a limp handshake, but he doesn't. Of course he doesn't. He's Mr Fucking Perfect.

I have to get away from here now before I say or do something that will make it harder for Erika to accept the fact that she's meant to be mine. I need her to see it in her own time, and if I tell this Aidan man to fuck off away from my girl, that process is going to take even longer.

"I should get going then," I say to Erika. "Now you have someone to help you get your things inside."

"I told you I am perfectly capable of pulling two suitcases by myself," Erika smiles.

Aidan doesn't give her a chance to prove it. He's taken the suitcase from me without me even registering what is happening. He isn't saying much, but he's looking at me with suspicion on his face. He knows Erika is meant to be mine. He knows I will take her back away from him.

"And this is why chivalry is dead," I laugh, focusing on Erika, refusing to look at Aidan.

She rolls her eyes and shakes her head.

"Thank you so much for your help today Jeremy," she says.

"Of course," I tell her. "Any time you need anything, you can call me."

Because Aidan here let you go back to the house you were attacked in alone. He would have let you clean up the mess alone. He would have let you walk through the streets alone, dragging your things behind you.

I lean in to kiss Erika's cheek. She stiffens slightly, but she lets me kiss her and she's still smiling when I stand back. The next time I do it, she won't stiffen. And soon, she'll be begging me to kiss her, and not just on the cheek.

"Should we go inside then?" Aidan asks Erika like I'm not even here.

Fucking Aidan.

Erika nods her head.

"See you around Jeremy," she says.

"Yeah, see you later," I reply and I start walking away, forcing myself not to look back.

See you around. See you fucking around. It's the sort of thing you say to someone who is barely an acquaintance. Someone you don't want to make plans to see. Someone you don't really want to see at all. After everything I've done for her today, I get a see you around.

I try to calm myself down as I walk. She didn't mean it. Not really. That was for Aidan's benefit. She obviously isn't ready to drop him quite yet and she wants him to think his place at her side is safe. Well it isn't. Not for much longer. Because I'm going to get my girl back. And I still stand by what I told Erika the night of the … mistake. If I can't have her, then no one can.

As I walk, I forget the brush off and instead, I start to picture the future with Erika being mine again. Now I just need a plan to make it happen. Now I know where she's living, it'll be so much easier. I can keep running into her, I can drop in on her and say I wanted to check that she's ok.

Obviously I'll be driving by her building regularly just to keep an eye on things. And I intend to find out more about this Aidan guy. In particular, I want to know where I can find him when he's not with Erika. Just in case he overstays his welcome and I have to give him a friendly warning to stay the fuck away from my girl.

Erika

What a strange day it's been so far. The last person I expected to see today was Jeremy, and if I had known in advance he was going to show up at my house, I wouldn't have gone back there. I would have said he was the last person I wanted to see. But strangely, I don't feel that way anymore.

I actually enjoyed having his company once I got used to the idea of him being there. And I feel like he has finally gotten the message that things are over between us. It was nice to see him just as a friend, and if I'm being honest, I felt a whole lot less nervous about being back at the house once I had someone with me.

At the same time, I was relieved when Aidan approached us outside of the apartment building. Jeremy was hanging around, clearly looking for an invite inside and something told me that wouldn't have been a good idea. For all he seemed to have gotten the message about us being over, I didn't want to give him any indication I had changed my mind about that and I thought it would be almost cruel to invite him right back into the thick of my life with no intentions of getting back with him. It would almost have felt like leading him on, giving him false hope.

I was glad to see Aidan for another reason too. Seeing him again sparked memories of the kiss we had shared and I could feel my pussy getting wet as I watched him approaching us. There was something so sexy about him, even when he was doing something as normal and every day as walking down the street.

Seeing the awkward interaction between Aidan and Jeremy was a little surprising. I kind of expected it from Jeremy – no doubt until I introduced Aidan as Nadia's brother, Jeremy was thinking there was something going on between Aidan and me, and he might have even been thinking it had started before we were over. It was Aidan's reaction that surprised me. The way he looked at Jeremy, he didn't so much look jealous as he did suspicious, like he didn't like Jeremy immediately at first sight. Maybe he was just jealous and I had read the signs wrong.

Once Jeremy left us, I turned to Aidan and beamed at him, Jeremy all but forgotten.

"What brings you here?" I ask. "Nadia's gone out."

I unlock the door to the apartment building as I say it and Aidan follows me inside and towards the elevator. The elevator car is already there and we get inside and I press the button for the third floor.

"It wasn't Nadia I came to see," Aidan says.

"Oh really?" I say, delighted to hear this.

"I just wanted to drop by and see how you were doing," he says.

We reach the third floor and the elevator doors ping open. We step out and head for the apartment.

"I'm ok," I say. "I've just come from the house. I went to get some of my things."

"With Jeremy?" he says quietly.

He is jealous. How can he be jealous of Jeremy? Of anyone? Doesn't he know how hot he is? Doesn't he know how he has an effect on me like no man has ever had before?

"Not really with him," I say as I unlock the apartment door and step inside. Aidan follows me and closes the door behind me. "He didn't know I wasn't staying at home. He called round to see if I was ok after he heard about the attack. It was good timing actually. He helped me get rid of all of the mess from the living room."

Aidan nods. He looks ready to ask another question, but I'm done talking about Jeremy. Jeremy is a part of my past and I'm hoping Aidan is going to be a part of my future. I see no reason for those two things to overlap. I get in the next sentence before Aidan can.

"Do you want to stay for dinner? It's nothing exciting, just jacket potatoes, but you're more than welcome to stay," I say.

"With an offer like that, how could I refuse," Aidan grins.

Feeling suddenly brave, I step closer to him and whisper in his ear, close enough to him for my breath to tickle his skin as I talk.

"If you thought that was a good offer, you want to see what we're having for dessert?" I ask.

AIDAN

I watch from my seat at the dining table as Erika chops up lettuce for the side salad. I offered to help her with dinner, but she wouldn't hear of it. After what she whispered in my ear when I told her I'd love to stay for dinner, I'm almost tempted to suggest skipping the main course and jumping right to dessert, but I don't. I like Erika and I want to take it slow with her. I don't want her to think I'm only after one thing, especially when the attack must have left her feeling a little vulnerable.

Although thoughts of what could happen between Erika and me now that we're alone in the apartment fill my mind with delicious images and make my cock ache for her, I just can't keep my mind from going back to Jeremy.

I know I showed more hostility towards him than I meant to, and I'll be honest. At first, that was because I was jealous when I saw Erika with him. But then he looked at me with such venom in his eyes that I started to take more notice. Even if he has a bit of a thing for Erika, she introduced me only as Nadia's brother, and that really didn't warrant such a look. It was like Jeremy felt like he owned Erika and I was muscling in on his territory. I didn't like it one bit. I was also a little bit disappointed that Erika introduced me as Nadia's brother, but really, what was she meant to say? This is Aidan, a guy I kissed?

There was something off about Jeremy. Something that gave me the creeps, and as a doctor, I have learned to read people pretty well over the years and I tend to trust my instincts. I don't want to say anything to Erika about it, because I could be way off, but something makes me think he's the one who attacked her.

That's not just based on the feeling I got when I first looked at him and when I shook his hand and he gripped my hand a little bit too tightly, like he had something to prove. No that would be crazy. I wasn't even considering it as a possibility until I noticed the scratches on the backs of Jeremy's hands. It could well be nothing. Maybe he has a cat, or maybe he works somewhere where that's likely to happen. But it also looked like those scratches could be consistent with someone choking someone and having that person claw at their hands in an attempt to get them off them.

I don't really know what to do with my suspicions. I don't want to tell Erika for two reasons. Firstly, I don't want her to think I'm some insanely jealous type who assumes any guy she talks to must be an awful person. Secondly, I don't want to worry her if I'm way off base with this. I know I can't go to the police with this either. Imagine me telling Officer Prescott my theory and her asking if I have any evidence of this, and I have to say well, I got a bad feeling about the guy and he had a couple of scratches on his hands so yeah, lock him up and throw away the key please.

I have to keep this to myself for now, but I will be keeping an eye out for Jeremy being around Erika too much. I might even mention it to Nadia, just so she can keep an eye on Erika if Jeremy comes here when I'm not around.

"Aidan? Are you ok? You've gone awfully quiet," Erika says as she comes towards the table with a plate in each hand.

I didn't realize how long I had been spaced out thinking about Jeremy and my suspicions, but she's finished making the dinner without me noticing. She puts the plates down, one in front of me and one in front of the chair beside mine which she pulls it out and sits down+.

"I'm fine," I smile. "Sorry. I was just in a world of my own there. These smell delicious."

She smiles at me and picks up her fork.

"They do smell good don't they?"

I begin to eat my potato, blowing on it when I see the steam billowing off it. I don't want to anger Erika by bringing Jeremy up again – she changed the subject pretty quickly when I was asking about him earlier – but I need to find out more about him to see if he seems like a shifty character or if I am just being jealous and looking for something that isn't there.

"So how do you know Jeremy?" I ask, aiming for a casual tone.

I think I must have missed the mark slightly when Erika glances at me out of the corner of her eye, a small smile of amusement curling her lips at the corners.

"Are you jealous Dr Miller?" she says.

"No," I laugh. "I'm just curious that's all."

I notice that she has avoided the question. Is that something she's done on purpose? Is she seeing Jeremy?

"You were just curious. Right, of course," she says, still with that smile.

She takes a bite of salad and chews it slowly and I'm starting to think that's the discussion over, but when she swallows, she starts to tell me about Jeremy and I realize she wasn't avoiding the question altogether, she was just taking a moment to wind me up. I kind of like that she does that. Or at least I would if it was about something less serious than the man who may have attacked her. I remind myself that might not be true, and even if it is, Erika has no idea that's why I'm asking her about him.

"Jeremy and I were dating for a while," she says. "It was nothing serious and I broke it off. Don't get me wrong, Jeremy is a nice guy and all, but there was just no spark between us you know? I knew it wasn't going anywhere and it seemed pointless dragging it out."

"And yet he still drops round to see you?" I ask.

I am sounding jealous now, but I guess it's better for now if Erika thinks I'm jealous rather than her maybe working out what I'm really thinking before I have any proof I am right.

"We said when we broke up we'd still be friends. To be honest, that's the first time I've seen him since we broke up," she tells me.

"It was quite recent then?" I ask.

"Yeah. It was about three or four days before the attack," she says. Her eyes widen for a moment and I think she's thinking the same thing as me. "Do you think whoever attacked me was watching me and knew I was alone because I had ended things with Jeremy?"

I really hadn't even considered that and it's clear to me that Erika most definitely isn't thinking the same thing as I'm thinking. And she said Jeremy is a nice guy. Maybe he is. Maybe I am all kinds of wrong about this. But still, the timing is a major coincidence, and her talking about someone watching her has given me another theory. What if Jeremy was watching the house so he knew exactly when Erika was in there alone? Maybe he wanted to know for sure just how much she remembered, and if she had remembered anything, he might have been planning on finishing the job. A shudder goes through me at that thought and I try to push it away, but it keeps nagging at me, even when Erika looks at me for an answer to her question.

"I don't know," I say honestly. "I mean I guess it's possible."

"Do you think I should call Officer Prescott and tell her I'd just split up with my boyfriend?" she asks.

Maybe I should say yes. Maybe that will get Jeremy onto Officer Prescott's radar. She might go to question him and get the same vibes as I did. She might see the scratches and make the same connection as I did. Before I can answer her question though, Erika is shaking her head.

"No. I can't do that. It might make the police suspect Jeremy," she says.

"Do you think there's any possibility …?" I start.

"No," Erika says, cutting me off before I can even finish the thought. "No. I don't. Jeremy wanted to get back with me. He wouldn't have hurt me."

"He wanted to get back with you?" I repeat.

She nods her head and that teasing little smile creeps back onto her face.

"Yeah, but you don't have to get all jealous again. I ended things with him for a reason and that reason still stands. Besides, he's finally taken the hint now. And I know we say we'll be friends, but that's just something you say isn't it? It just means if we see each other on the street, we'll be civil to each other. It doesn't mean we're going to be real friends that see each other socially."

"The last girl I dated seriously was in medical school, and that was a good few years ago now, so I'll have to take your word for that one," I grin.

I have to let go of the Jeremy questions for now before Erika starts to think I'm one of those possessive nut jobs that won't let a girl they like have any sort of life of her own.

"It's been that long since you've been in a relationship?" Erika says.

"Yeah. We broke up and then I got my first internship. Don't get me wrong, I've had flings and stuff since then, but I have always told myself I didn't have time for a girlfriend," I say. I pause for a moment and look at Erika as I say the next part. "The truth is I had just never found a girl special enough to make me want to make time for a girlfriend. Until now."

Erika's cheeks flush slightly and she smiles at me. She doesn't say anything, but I can see she's pleased with my words. After a few seconds, she looks back at her plate and scoops up the last forkful of her potato. I have already finished mine and she's still chewing as she stands up and begins to collect the dishes up.

"You've barely finished eating," I point out.

"I know," she says after she swallows. "But Nadia's apartment is so tidy. I don't want to leave a mess."

"I wasn't suggesting we leave the dishes here for Nadia to clean up," I laugh. "Just that you actually finish your dinner before you start washing the dishes."

She laughs with me but she makes no effort to come back to the table. Instead, she starts filling the sink with hot water and dish soap. I get up and move into the kitchen area beside her, grabbing a drying towel.

"You don't have to do that," she says. "You're a guest."

"I'm a guest that has house manners. You see, I want to be invited back," I tell her.

"Right, well let's see what your drying skills are like and we'll see if that's likely," Erika grins.

I laugh and nudge her hip with mine.

"I'm an expert with a drying towel," I tell her.

She hands me the first plate and raises an eyebrow, watching me. I make a show of drying the plate to perfection. Erika goes back to washing.

"Ok, you can come again," she says.

We get through the dishes in no time. There was hardly any to do. I stand with my ass leaning back against the counter as

Erika goes and wipes down the dining room table. I watch her ass as she bends slightly at the waist. God she looks good. She comes back to the kitchen, flashing me a smile as she does it. She begins to wipe down the counter top opposite me and I can't resist her any longer. I have to hold her. Touch her. Kiss her.

I cross the kitchen and wrap my arms around her waist. She gives a surprised laugh and covers my arms with hers. I nuzzle my face against her neck.

"So how about that dessert then?" I say.

"I think there's some ice cream in the freezer," she grins.

"Not really what I had in mind," I say, nibbling on her ear lobe.

"There might be some cake somewhere."

I kiss down her neck.

"Nope. Still not what I'm craving."

"And what might that be?" she asks.

I release my hold on her long enough to spin her in my arms and then I pull her tightly against me, my arms around her waist.

"This," I say before I press my lips against hers.

Her lips part and her arms wrap around my neck as she melts into me. She feels so small and fragile in my arms, but she acts anything but fragile. She pushes her hands into my hair, mashing my lips more tightly against hers and pushing her tongue into my mouth. I move my hands up and down her back, pushing them beneath her top so I can feel her bare skin. I want to feel every inch of her bare skin, run my hands over it, my tongue over it. I want to make Erika come so hard she forgets all about Jeremy. Except I think it's me that's the one still thinking about him. Ok then, I want to make Erika come so hard I forget all about Jeremy. Either way is good with me as long as Erika enjoys what I am going to do to her.

I move my hands to her bra and unclasp it, bringing my hands around to the front of her body and cupping her breasts. She makes a muffled moaning sound against my lips as I work her nipples between my fingers. Her nipples harden almost instantly between my fingers and she arches her back slightly as I roll them and goose bumps scurry over her skin.

I move my lips from hers kissing down her neck, being careful to be gentle in that area this time. My kisses are feather light, barely even touching Erika's skin and she moans again, a sound full of frustration and longing.

I pull my hands away from her breasts and out of her t-shirt. I bring them up and push her t-shirt off her shoulder, running my tongue over the bare skin of her shoulder blades. I run my hands down her body, pausing at the waist band of her jeans and opening her button and lower the zipper. I push her jeans down and then her panties and then I cup her ass with my hands and lift her, placing her in a sitting position on the edge of the kitchen counter. I step between her legs and kiss her mouth again as I run my fingers over her lips and find her clit. She is so wet that I gasp a little as the feel of her sends shivers of lust through me.

She wraps her legs around my waist as I massage her clit with my fingers, our lips still locked together. Erika's hands roam over my back, my sides, like she wants to feel all of me. She presses herself against me, her breasts pressing against my chest. She moves her hips, writhing against my fingers.

She pulls her lips from mine and presses her face into my neck, lightly nipping the skin there between her teeth. She is gasping and panting as she does it and the heat of her breath on my neck sends hot waves through my body and down to my cock.

My cock is rock hard, aching to be inside of Erika, but I am going to hold myself back until I have made her come. Only then will I enter her.

She sounds close now and I slow down my movement. Erika pulls back from me slightly, frowning as I slow my movement right down to an almost stop. I barely graze her clit with my fingers now, teasing her, drawing this out. She bucks her hips, trying to get some pressure on her clit but I anticipate her move and snatch my fingers away at the last second.

Erika looks at me, her chest rising and falling in time with her gasping breaths. I smile at her and then I run my hands over her thighs and gently disentangle her legs from around me. I kneel down, and pull Erika right to the edge of the counter, and then I bury my face in her mound.

She is all I can smell, all I can taste. I lick her, drinking in her juices, barely able to stop myself from pulling her free of the counter and fucking her right here on the kitchen floor.

I lick her harder, faster. Erika presses her pussy against my face, gasping and moaning as I bring her right back to the edge. I suck her clit into my mouth, nipping it lightly between my lips and then I release it and press down on it, moving it from side to side beneath my tongue.

Erika's moans become louder and more agonized sounding as I keep working her, not relenting for a second. I feel her clit begin to pulse against my tongue as a rush of liquid erupts from her. Her moan becomes my name, her voice dripping with lust as she says it. Even as she orgasms hard, I don't let up on her for a second. I keep working her with my tongue and I reach up and push two fingers inside of her.

Feeling the slippery warmth of her wrapping around my fingers almost pushes me over the edge myself, but I swallow back the feelings, wanting to concentrate only on Erika. I move my fingers in and out of Erika in the same rhythm I use to keep licking her clit.

She's going wild now, her whole body shuddering as waves of pleasure coast through her body. She is no longer saying my name. Her breath comes in a series of tiny gasps that she releases as whimpers. I feel her muscles tensing and she sucks in a deep breath and holds it.

I press down on her g-spot with my fingers and her clit with my tongue at the same time. She lets out the breath she was holding in a scream that sounds almost like an animal sound. That sound sends a wave of desire through me and I can't wait any longer. I have to have her.

I slip my fingers out of her and pull my face away from her pussy. I sit back on my heels and admire her for a second. Her pussy is dark red, flushed from her orgasm and I can see the moisture beading on her lips. The sight of her takes my breath away and when I push myself to my feet, I can feel my legs shaking.

Erika is leaning back on her palms, her eyes squeezed tight shut, her face contorted. Her chest heaves as she pants. I imagine what her breasts will look like when I get her out of her t-shirt and I feel another pulse of desire go through my cock.

She opens her eyes as her breathing begins to go back to normal. She looks at me beneath eyelids heavy with lust.

"Wow," she smiles.

I smile back at her and step back between her legs and kiss her again. Our kiss is deep and passionate, our tongues colliding, massaging, and tumbling against each other. Her lips feel like they were made to fit mine and her body against me feels like I have been waiting my whole life for this moment.

I run my hands down Erika's back as her hands move around my body and begin to undo my belt. She fumbles it open and then she starts on the button of my jeans. I am so turned on I almost come as she brushes her hand over the front of my jeans, rubbing the denim over my cock.

She gets the button open and then the zipper. She pushes my jeans and boxer shorts down. I pull her closer to me, ready to plunge into her warmth and feel her tight little pussy wrapped around my cock. I line myself up, and as I am about to slam into her, I hear a key going into the front door.

Erika hears it at the exact same moment as I do.

"Shit. Nadia," she says.

I jump back from her and begin to fasten my jeans and belt back up. Erika pushes herself off the counter, as graceful as a cat. She yanks her jeans back up and fastens them and begins to try to tame down her hair. I can't help but smile when she grabs a cloth and begins to wash the place she was sitting on the counter. Nadia comes in as she's washing the counter top down.

"Hi," she says. "Oh hi Aidan, I didn't know you were here. I'm not interrupting anything am I?"

"No," Erika and I both say together.

Nadia smiles knowingly.

"So yes then," she says with a soft laugh. "Let me just grab a glass of water and then I'll get out of your hair."

Erika gives me a pleading look. A look that I can read easily enough. Please don't let this be a thing that gets awkward.

"Honestly Nadia, you're not interrupting anything. I just came over to see how Erika was feeling and we had dinner together," I say.

"Yeah," Erika puts in. "You should have been a few minutes earlier and you could have interrupted the washing up. I'm sure Aidan would have been pleased about that."

"I would have," I confirm with a grin.

I'm not sure whether Nadia is buying the bullshit we're selling her, but she smiles and relaxes slightly, leaning against the countertop. If she doesn't believe us, she's at least going to pretend she does and that will have to do.

I have to bite my lip to keep myself from smiling when I see Erika's cheeks start to flush as Nadia leans against the spot on the counter that Erika was coming in only moments ago. Erika turns away quickly and starts wiping down the counter behind her, even though it's already clean. Nadia smiles.

"If you clean like this every time you make dinner, I think I'm going to enjoy having you around Erika," she laughs.

"You'll definitely enjoy having me around then," Erika says. "I'm a bit of a clean freak to be honest."

AIDAN

I want Erika so badly that it's like a physical ache inside of me. I can't believe Nadia came home when she did. I mean who goes out for a night out and comes home at like ten o'clock. Only my fucking sister apparently. If she had just been like fifteen minutes later, but no.

I really wanted to just keep quiet and let her get her glass of water and go to her bedroom or whatever she was planning on doing to give Erika and me some space. We could have then gone to Erika's room and finished what we started. But I saw the look Erika was giving me and I knew that she didn't want that. I can understand her point. It's only her first full day living there – she probably feels like it's too early to be chasing Nadia out of the shared space. And maybe she's a bit embarrassed with Nadia being my sister.

Whatever her reasoning, I know she was uncomfortable with the idea of letting Nadia just slip back away and so I made out there was nothing to interrupt. I feel like I've done the right thing, but my God am I frustrated inside. My whole body is tingling, still filled with desire for Erika. I have never met a woman who can affect me the way Erika can. I love that she has this effect on me, but right now, I hate it. I want to be able to think straight for a second, but all I can think about is how her clit pulsed against my tongue as she came. How she moaned my name. How she tasted, how she smelled.

I blink away the images and sit down at the table listening to Nadia and Erika discussing their cleaning habits. They really are perfectly suited to living together as they both like things clean and tidy. Nadia makes some coffee and the three of us go through to the living room with it.

The atmosphere between us is friendly but I suspect that Nadia knows she did interrupt something and I think she'll try and go off to bed quickly, but I also know that nothing is going to happen between Erika and me tonight now. I think Erika would prefer if I left her and Nadia to it, but I don't know how to sneak off before Nadia feels like she's in the way without it looking like I'm just leaving because I'm not going to get sex.

It's actually Erika who gives me a way out.

"Are you both working tomorrow then?" she asks.

"I am," Nadia says. "I work every week, Monday to Friday."

"I am too," I say. "In fact, I'm starting at five, so I think I might call it a night if you two ladies don't mind."

They both shake their heads no and I swallow down the rest of my coffee and stand up.

"I'll see you out," Erika says, standing up too.

I nod and she follows me out into the hallway. I open the apartment door and Erika steps into the corridor with me. The second we're out of the apartment, we look at each other and burst into laughter.

"Shit, that was close," Erika says.

"I know," I agree. "If she'd turned up five minutes earlier, we probably wouldn't have even heard her coming in."

"Imagine if she'd walked in on us like that. Especially on a kitchen counter. She'd have had me kicked out and the bleach out within seconds," Erika laughs.

"Not to mention the three of us would probably all have been scarred for life by the experience," I add with a grin.

Erika nods and laughs. I lean in and kiss her. I kiss her lips, but it's a quick kiss. Anything else and my cock will be hard and wanting to take things further again within seconds.

"I'll call you tomorrow when I've finished work ok?" I say.

Erika nods.

"Goodnight," she says.

"Oh it was," I say, although I know that's not what she meant.

Her smile widens and I kiss her again quickly and then I turn and walk away before I can change my mind. I get into the elevator and go down, smiling to myself thinking about tonight. Erika really is amazing and even though I've just left her, I already can't wait to see her again.

The elevator doors ping open and I step out into the lobby. I cross it and leave the building, being sure to pull the front door behind me until I hear it click closed. The night air is cold now and I pause to pull up the zipper on my jacket. As I fasten the zipper, I get a cold shiver down my back and I feel the hairs standing up on the back of my neck, like someone is watching me. I glance around but I can't see anyone. I shake my head. What the hell is wrong with me? I'm not normally paranoid like this.

Just as I dismiss the feeling, a slight movement across the road from where I'm standing catches my eye. I squint slightly, peering through the darkness and I see him. A man is sitting in a black car opposite me. I keep looking at him until my eyes adjust to the darkness a little more.

I can't see his face. His collar is pulled up and he's wearing a baseball cap pulled down low, but somehow, I know he's staring back at me, our eyes locked on each other's. And somehow, I know exactly who it is. Jeremy. He's watching the building, watching for Erika.

I take a step forward, unsure of exactly what I'm going to say or do, especially if I get to the car and find out I'm mistaken about who is driving it. As I reach the curb, the engine of the black car roars to life and it pulls away too quickly, the tires squealing. Only when the car reaches the intersection at the end of the block do the headlights come on.

Now I'm sure I was right about the driver being Jeremy, or at the very least being someone who was up to no good. If it was all a coincidence and it was just a stranger waiting for someone from one of the buildings, they wouldn't have had that reaction to me approaching. They would have just assumed I was walking that way. And who goes to those extremes to hide their faces if they're not up to no good?

I run to my car, determined to follow the black car and see for sure if the driver is Jeremy or not, but by the time I get in and get the car started and blast down to the intersection, there is no sign of the black car.

I punch the steering wheel in frustration as I head towards home. I tell myself its ok now. Even if it was Jeremy, he's gone now and Erika is safe at home with Nadia. I remind myself again to have a chat with Nadia and warn her about Jeremy so she doesn't inadvertently put Erika in danger by letting him into the apartment.

I drive the rest of the way home, go inside and shower and go to bed. I really do have an early start in the morning, but still, sleep isn't coming and I don't think it will be anytime soon either. My mind is swirling with images of Erika and her gorgeous body, and in between the nice images, darker images swirl, images of Jeremy and the lengths he might go to so that he can keep Erika and me apart.

I have finished my second round of the day and checked new patients in and discharged old ones. And through it all, I have never once stopped thinking about Erika. I am sitting in the break room now, drinking the last few mouthfuls of an almost cold cup of coffee and thinking about her once more. I have to have her. I just have to. I'm going to drive myself insane if I don't see her again soon.

I can hardly wait for my shift to be over so I can call her. I hope she's free tonight. I really need to see her. I'm going to ask her to come over to my place. At least there, there's no one to interrupt us. I hope she says yes. She might not though. She might have other plans, or she might feel uncomfortable coming to my place.

I feel like a nervous teenager about to ask his crush to go to the prom the way my mind keeps trying to shake my confidence, telling me that Erika isn't going to want to come over tonight. Or maybe ever. Maybe she was glad of the interruption. I tell myself that's nonsense. She was as into it last night as I was and she was as disappointed as me when Nadia brought a swift end to our night.

"Hi Aidan," a voice says, pulling me out of my thoughts, but not managing to completely remove the images of Erika from my mind. "I wondered where you had got to."

"Hey Stacy," I say. I nod down to my cup. "Just trying to grab my first drink of the last eight hours."

"Ugh, tell me about it," she replies, pouring herself a cup of coffee from the coffee pot and coming to sit down next to me. "It's bedlam out there today isn't it?"

"Isn't every day?" I laugh.

She nods her head and smiles.

"It sure is. Five o'clock can't come soon enough, but I don't want to seem too eager in case I jinx myself and end up with a rush and have to stay back," she says.

I know that feeling. It always seems that on the days you really need to get away, something comes up that keeps you back. And it's not the sort of job you can just walk away from when your shift has ended. If something goes wrong, there's an unwritten rule that says all hands stay on deck until things stabilize.

"Same here," I agree.

"You finish at five too?" she says.

I nod my head and she smiles.

"Ok, how about this? If we both get away on time, we'll go and grab a drink in the bar across the road to celebrate a successful escape," she says.

"Ah, I can't sorry," I say. "I have plans tonight."

"No worries. Maybe another time?" she says.

I nod although I have no intentions of actually doing it. I want to spend the little bit of time I get to myself with Erika, not the people I work with all day.

"What are your big plans then?" she asks. When I don't respond quickly enough, she gives me a conspiratorial smile. "You have a date?"

I shrug and she takes it as a yes.

"With someone from the hospital?"

I shake my head. Erika is nothing to do with the hospital now and I'm not about to tell Stacy my date – assuming Erika agrees to it – is with an ex-patient.

"Make the most of it then," Stacy laughs. "You know as well as I do that if you're not dating someone who gets the long hours and the cancelled plans, it won't last."

"Thanks for the vote of confidence," I say with a smile.

I smile, but I have to wonder if she's right. No, of course she isn't right. It's hard to date a doctor because of the reasons she mentioned, but plenty of the other staff here are married or in serious relationships with people who don't work in a hospital themselves.

"It's nothing personal," Stacy grins. "I just think you'd have a better chance of it working out if you dated, say, a nurse."

I really don't want to sit here and listen to all of the reasons Erika and I won't work out. I swallow down a mouthful more of my coffee, wincing at how cold it is, and I stand up.

"You're probably right," I say.

I tip the rest of the coffee out of the cup and then rinse it out in the sink.

"Catch you later," I say heading out of the break room.

I walk towards my office wondering if Stacy is right. Are Erika and I destined to fail? I really hope not, but what Stacy said is true. It's hard for people who work to live rather than live to work to understand the long hours, the being on call, the dropping everything for work when I need to. But some people do get it, and what's to say Erika isn't one of them?

I know I shouldn't let Stacy get into my head. She loves a bit of drama and if there's nothing going on, she tends to create something and I guess today's a quiet day and she chose my potential relationship with Erika to be her drama.

Or maybe she wants you two to not work out because she has a thing for you, a little voice inside of my head whispers.

I guess that could be true, but I find it unlikely. Yes, Stacy flirts with me. She always has since she started working here, but she probably flirts with everyone like that. It's just a bit of fun. And I've never said or done anything to give her the impression I'm interested in being anything but friends with her, so what would be the point in her trying to split Erika and me up before we even really get going?

I'm being paranoid. She was most likely just making conversation. Nothing more sinister than that. And I'm blowing it up into this big thing. God I must be really into Erika to let her get so far into my head that the thought of us not going the distance throws me into turmoil like this.

The last part of my shift drags like crazy. All I can think about is calling Erika, hearing her voice, her laugh. And hopefully getting to see her tonight.

My shift finally ends and I waste no time in getting out of there before anyone can ask me to take a quick look at something and I end up stuck at work for another couple of hours.

I go down to the parking lot and get into my car and drive away. It's only once I'm off the hospital grounds that I fully relax. I drive home and go inside. I'm whistling to myself as I kick my shoes off and sit down. I pull my phone out and smile as I scroll through my contacts and find Erika's name. I hit call and she answers the phone quickly.

"Hi you," she says.

"Hi," I reply. "How's things?"

"Good," Erika says. "Boring but good. I miss work."

"Just wait until you're back. Within a day or two you'll be wishing you were off again," I say.

"Yeah you're probably right," Erika laughs. "How was your day?"

"Not bad," I say. "I managed to actually finish on time and that's always a win."

Erika laughs softly down the phone and I imagine I can feel her breath on my ear. The feeling makes me ache for her.

"I was wondering if you fancied coming over to my place tonight?" I say. "I thought we could order in and maybe watch a movie or something."

My heart races while I wait for Erika to indignantly tell me she doesn't want to come to my place.

"Sounds good," she says instead. "What time?"

I resist the urge to punch the air with my fist and instead I just grin to myself.

"I'll pick you up around eight o'clock," I say.

"Great. Eight o'clock it is," Erika says.

We chat for a bit longer and then we hang up saying we'll see each other at eight o'clock and have nothing left for us to talk about. That wouldn't be the worst thing in the world. Sometimes there are more interesting things to do than talk. Especially when the person you're with is as gorgeous and sexy as Erika is.

I scroll through my contacts again and settle on Nadia's name. My thumb hovers over it, ready to hit call, but at the last second, I change my mind and come out of my contacts and put my phone down.

It's not Nadia's job to look after Erika and I don't want to freak her out by letting her think some nut job might try to force his way into her apartment at any given moment. It's not like anything can happen tonight anyway; Erika is going to be at my place and if Jeremy tries anything here, I'll keep Erika safe.

Besides, the more I think about it, the more I think I massively overreacted last night. It was most likely all just a coincidence. It was probably someone dropping off a friend or a girlfriend and making sure they got inside safely. Once they did, the driver had no reason to hang around and so they sped off. The roads were quiet enough to get away with it and the driver might have just wanted to get home quickly and get an early night.

Whoever it was definitely watched me for a moment before speeding off though. But when I think about it, I was staring into the car. If I was parked somewhere and some guy came out of a building and stood staring into my car, I'm sure I would watch them to see if they were up to no good too.

Yes, that's likely all it was. As if it would be Jeremy. I'm still going to be extra vigilant for the next few days and try to make sure Erika isn't wandering the streets alone, but I know it's likely all for nothing.

Maybe Erika was right. Maybe I'm just jealous and I'm concocting this whole theory just to justify why I have bad feelings about Jeremy instead of just admitting I'm worried Erika decides to blow me off and take him back instead.

Whatever is going on, for the moment, I need to stop over thinking everything and concentrate on cleaning up around the place a bit. I don't want Erika to come over and think I'm some sort of slob. I smile to myself as I think of her telling Nadia she's a bit of a cleaning freak. My place is clean and reasonably tidy, but I still think I have a bit of work to do if I want to impress Erika. And I really, really do want to impress her.

ERIKA

I can barely keep the smile off my face as I end the call. Aidan has invited me over to his place for dinner and a movie tonight and I know what that means. At Aidan's place, there won't be anyone to disturb us right at the crucial moment.

I've thought of nothing but Aidan and how good he made my body feel since last night, and now I know I have it all to look forward to again tonight. Knowing I'll soon be seeing Aidan leaves me feeling excited and tingly, but it also leaves me free to think about something else. Now I know it's going to happen for real tonight, I don't need to spend every second imagining what it will be like to have Aidan inside of me.

I suddenly remember I meant to call Officer Prescott and tell her that nothing seemed to have been stolen from my house. I grab my phone and go to my room and find Officer Prescott's card. I type the number into my phone, hit call, and listen to the phone ringing.

"Officer Prescott," Officer Prescott says curtly as she answers my call.

I am thrown for a moment. I was really expecting to get her voicemail for some reason, and I am left momentarily mute when she comes on the line.

"Hello?" she says.

"Umm, hi. It's Erika Hart," I say.

"Oh hi Erika, is everything ok?" Officer Prescott says.

She sounds less curt and more like how I remembered her to sound now; calm and efficient but not cold.

"Yes, everything's fine," I say quickly.

"Did your memory of the incident come back?" she asks.

"No, unfortunately not," I say. God I wish it had. "I just wanted to let you know I stopped by the house to collect some things yesterday and I had a look around, and nothing has been taken. You asked me to let you know either way."

"Yes, I remember," Officer Prescott says. "And you're certain nothing has gone?"

"Yeah," I say. "To be honest, there was very little worth stealing, but what was worth stealing is still there."

"Ok, well thank you for letting me know," Officer Prescott says.

"Do you have anything?" I ask, fearing I already know the answer. If the police knew who had done this to me, they would have been in touch with me by now. "Do you have any suspects?"

"Unfortunately not," Officer Prescott replies. "As you know, we have the DNA sample, but there have been no matches in our system. And none of your neighbors had anything to tell us that could help. We're still trying to find more CCTV cameras in the area and get access to the footage, but as of yet, we haven't got anything close enough to establish that anyone on the footage was even heading to your street, let alone your house."

It's not good news, but at least it shows that the police are taking this seriously and are at least trying to get to the bottom of it.

"I appreciate it even though you don't have much to go on," I say.

"Thank you," Officer Prescott says. "We are still doing everything we can to catch your attacker, and as always, if you remember anything, no matter how small, don't hesitate to call ok?"

"I won't. Thank you," I say.

"You're welcome. Have a good day," Officer Prescott says.

She ends the call before I can respond. I knew if the police had any leads they would have called me, and I knew that the chances of them finding my attacker without my memories coming back where slim to none. I had accepted that. And yet, somehow, talking to Officer Prescott and having it confirmed that they have no idea who did this to me somehow makes me feel a little bit down.

I decide to call Jennifer. She always knows what to say to cheer me up, and besides I want to tell her about last night with Aidan and tell her about what I hope will happen tonight. I've kept her up to date with my huge crush on him and the fact that we kissed on the day I moved into this place and Jennifer was really excited for me. She's going to freak when she hears the latest development.

"Aidan asked me to go over to his place to have dinner tonight," I blurt out the second Jennifer answers her phone.

"Hi Erika," Jennifer laughs.

"Hi," I say, grinning. "So Aidan asked me to go over to his place to have dinner tonight."

"It's about time," Jennifer says.

"Well actually we had dinner together at Nadia's place last night as well," I say. "And not just dinner. We were fooling around, and just before we actually got to have sex, Nadia came home and almost caught us."

"So? Yeah Aidan is her brother but he's a grown man. Surely you don't have to hide this from her?" Jennifer says.

"No you don't understand," I say. "She literally almost caught us. We were in the kitchen at the time."

Jennifer bursts into laughter and I join in. Instantly my worries about the police investigation begin to dissipate. The situation with it is no better and no worse than it was yesterday and I wasn't upset about it then, so why start upsetting myself about it now?

"What are youthinking?" Jennifer laughs. "I take it the invite for dinner is more code for come and have sex somewhere we won't be disturbed then."

"I hope so," I laugh. "Mind you, I am kind of hungry. I wouldn't say no to dinner first."

"Well at least you've got your priorities right," Jennifer says.

"I thought so," I agree.

"So are you nervous?" Jennifer asks.

"A little bit," I admit. "I'm not nervous about being around Aidan. I guess I'm more nervous I'll screw it up between us before it's even really gotten going."

"You won't. Just be your usual charming self," Jennifer says.

I can't decide if she's being sarcastic or not, but it's not bad advice. The first few times Aidan saw me I was in a hospital gown, my hair not brushed, I probably stunk and I know I looked damned rough. And yet he still liked me enough to want to keep seeing me after I was discharged. So maybe he did like me just being myself. Ok, I can do that.

"Huh?" I say when I realise Jennifer is still talking.

"I said if that doesn't work, then move on. You don't need to be with someone who doesn't like you for who you are," she says.

"I know that," I say.

"Do you?" Jennifer asks.

"Umm, yeah," I say, confused as to where this is going. "Why?"

"Just don't let Aidan do a Jeremy on you," Jennifer says.

"What do you mean by that?" I ask.

"You know, try to like keep you away from your friends and stuff," Jennifer says.

"Jeremy never did that. We both preferred to stay home," I

say. "But speaking of Jeremy, there's something else I need to tell you. He's finally taken the hint about us being over."

"Yeah you said he'd stopped texting and calling you," Jennifer replies.

"No, better than that," I say. "I went back to the house yesterday to collect some stuff and I started trying to clean up the mess in the living room. Jeremy dropped by while I was there. I was wary at first, but he said he'd heard what had happened and just wanted to make sure I was ok. He helped me sort out the mess and he admitted he had gone a bit too far with the messages and that, but that he got it now."

Jennifer doesn't say anything and I start to think we've been cut off.

"Jen?" I say.

"Yeah, I'm here. Sorry, the line went weird for a moment. That's brilliant news. Now if you want my advice, forget all about Jeremy and go get yourself that hot doctor," she says.

"Done and done," I reply with a laugh.

I take one final look in the mirror before I leave my room. I don't want to get too dressed up to go to Aidan's place and look over dressed, but I really want to look nice for tonight, and in the end, I settled on a short, flowy black dress that I think strikes the right balance between casual and dressy. I decided to leave my hair down and I added a pair of diamante earrings.

When I walk into the living room, Nadia whistles when she sees me.

"You like the dress?" I ask.

"Yeah it's gorgeous," she says. "Where are you off to?"

"I'm going for dinner at Aidan's place," I say, feeling myself blushing slightly.

Nadia beams.

"That's fantastic, you two are great together," she says. She grimaces suddenly. "Dammit. I did interrupt something yesterday didn't I? You should have said and I would have gotten out of the way."

"Honestly, you didn't," I say.

Nadia raises an eyebrow and I laugh.

"Ok, you did. But it's your place Nadia. I wasn't about to tell you to make yourself scarce."

"Well next time Aidan's over here, just let me know and I'll stay out a bit later," she laughs.

"Deal," I smile.

The intercom buzzes and Nadia claps her hands together.

"That'll be Aidan," she says. I nod and head towards the door. "Have fun."

"I will," I say.

I pull the door open.

"Don't worry. I won't wait up," Nadia calls after me.

I can still hear her laughing as I pull the door shut and head down to the lobby. I can see Aidan on the other side of the glass door. He's wearing dark blue jeans and a white shirt and he looks effortlessly delicious. A shiver of desire goes through me as I see his eyes going up and down me. Finally, his eyes settle on my face and he smiles at me. I return his smile as I pull the door open and step outside.

"You look amazing," Aidan says as we walk to his car and he opens the door for me.

"Thanks," I smile as I get in.

Aidan closes the door behind me and walks around the front of the car. He's looking around as though he's looking for someone and I peer out of the windows but I can't see anyone. Aidan gets in the car.

"Who were you looking for?" I ask.

"Huh?" he says.

"You looked like you were looking for someone," I say. "When you were walking around the car."

"Oh. I thought I heard someone shouting at me. I must be going mad," he smiles as he pulls away from the curb and joins the steady flow of traffic.

Something tells me he's lying, but I tell myself I'm being ridiculous. Why would he have lied about that? And who could he possibly have been looking for that he wouldn't have just told me about?

"So what are we having for dinner then?" I ask.

"I've got a pizza delivery booked for eight thirty," he says. "I hope that's ok."

"It's perfect," I say. "I love pizza."

"And then for dessert, I thought maybe we could have the same as we had last night," he says, giving me a sideways glance and winking at me.

"Sounds good. Should I call Nadia and tell her to drop by at about half past nine just so it's authentic?" I joke.

Aidan groans and shakes his head.

"Don't even go there," he laughs.

"I told her I was coming to your place tonight. I hope that's ok," I say.

Aidan nods.

"Sure. I would have told her the truth last night and told her to go back out or something, but I got the impression you were a bit uncomfortable," he says.

"It just didn't feel right asking her for privacy so soon after moving in," I admit.

"Yeah I understand," Aidan says. He grins again. "But that won't be a problem tonight. You can have as much dessert as you want tonight. Assuming you want any of course."

"Oh I was thinking a nice big helping of dessert is exactly what I need," I say.

I bite the inside of my lip to keep from smiling when Aidan groans and shuffles in his seat. I am pleased to see that I can have such a profound effect on him. I am not unaffected myself though. This conversation is making me crave Aidan's touch more and more, and its hard work not to touch him right now. I keep my hands to myself though. It'll be worth the wait. He'll be worth the wait.

I swallow the last mouthful of my pizza and wipe my mouth on a napkin.

"That was delicious," I say.

Aidan nods his head, still finishing up his last slice.

"Cooking isn't my forte, but damn I know how to choose a good take away place," he says.

"Do you never cook?" I ask.

"Not really," he says. "Usually by the time I've finished work, I can't be bothered so I either grab a sandwich from the canteen at work or I get something on the way home. I do occasionally stretch to making a bacon sandwich now and again though."

"Fancy," I grin.

Aidan laughs and stands up from the table.

"Should we go through to the living room?" he says.

I nod my head and follow him through to the living room. His place is every bit as nice as I imagined it would be. His living room is dominated by a huge cream leather three piece suite arranged to face a large flat screen TV. Behind the couch is a large wall made all of glass that looks out onto his balcony and then over the city beyond it.

"I can't believe you sit with your back to that view," I smile as we sit down on the couch.

"But if I turned the couch around, then the TV would be upset," Aidan says.

We both laugh and I shake my head at him. He switches the TV on and flicks through the movie channels.

"What do you fancy?" he asks.

You, I think to myself.

"Anything except a western," I say.

Aidan flicks through the channels a few more times and finds a drama about a missing girl that's due to start and we settle on that channel.

"Would you like a drink or anything?" Aidan asks me.

"No I'm ok thanks," I say. "But for the record, you don't have to try and get me drunk to have your way with me."

Aidan laughs.

"That wasn't my intention, but now that you mention it …"

He shuffles closer to me across the couch and presses his lips to mine. I reach up and push my hands into his hair as his kiss deepens. My body comes to life, my clit tingling, my pussy wet, my skin craving Aidan's touch. He wraps his arms around my waist pulling me closer to him. I move with him, straddling him. He pushes his hands up inside of my dress, his nails tracing little circles on my thighs and making goose bumps run up and down my legs.

I reach for the hem of my dress and lift it, pulling my lips away from Aidan's long enough to pull the dress over my head and throw it to one side. Our lips come back together as Aidan moves his hands over my back. He unhooks my bra and teases it down my arms, tossing it down onto the ground with my dress.

I push my tongue into his mouth as I begin to open the buttons on his shirt. When I have them all open, I push the shirt down off his arms and it joins my clothes. I break my lips from Aidan's for long enough to admire his naked chest and stomach. The sight of his perfect six pack and his toned pecs sends another wash of desire through me and I find his lips with my own again.

Aidan runs his hands up and down my body, over my back, my sides, leaving behind a trail of tingling fire that leaves me wanting more. He moves his hands around the front of my body and kneads my breasts, bringing my nipples to attention. He moves one hand lower, running his fingers over my stomach and pushing them into my panties. He finds my clit and begins to work it, slowly, almost lazily.

Within seconds his feather light touch has me soaking wet and needing more. I press down, grinding myself against Aidan's hand and into his lap beneath it. He pulls his mouth from mine and kisses my neck as his fingers tease me.

He moves his fingers from my clit, moving them back up to my breasts. I keep grinding into his lap. I can feel his hard cock through his jeans and I can't help but gasp in a sigh of delight when I feel how big it is. I need to feel him inside of me. Now. I reach down and begin to open Aidan's jeans.

Once they're open, he lifts his ass and I tug them down to his thighs, followed by his boxer shorts. He drags them further, kicking them away. I grab his hard cock in my fist and begin to move my hand up and down his length. He moans as I move my hand slowly, teasing him.

He begins to thrust his hips, forcing me to up my pace. I work with him, moving my hand faster until he grabs my wrist and lifts my hand away from him. He looks into my eyes for a moment and then he cups my ass with his hands and flips me so I end up laying on my back on the couch with him kneeling between my legs.

Aidan looks down at me with eyes heavy with lust. I strain my neck up towards him, reaching for him and grabbing his shoulders, pulling him down to me. He leans down without resistance, fitting his mouth over mine once more. He reaches between us with one hand and pulls my panties down. I kick them free and wrap my legs around his waist as his tongue massages mine.

He kisses me until I'm breathless and then he pulls back and reaches between us, lining his cock up with my pussy. He slams inside of me, his cock stretching my pussy until it's almost painful. I cry out as he fills me and tingles spread up through my pussy and into my stomach. Aidan begins to thrust his hips, moving deliciously inside of me, and I move with him, matching his eager thrusts with equally eager thrusts of my own.

I can feel my stomach contracting and my pussy tightening as waves of pleasure spread out through my body. Each thrust makes me cry out as the pleasure intensifies, throbbing through me. I can feel my climax rushing closer and I welcome it, moving my hips faster, drawing it out.

I call out Aidan's name as my climax washes over me like a tidal wave, crashing through my body and leaving me unable to breath for a moment. My body tingles and sparks, and my pussy throbs again, tightening around Aidan's cock, making my orgasm even more intense.

As my orgasm starts to fade, I find I can breathe again, and I wrap my arms around Aidan's shoulders, clinging to him, panting for breath, as he keeps pumping into me. He ups the pace and I know he's close to his own orgasm. His breathing is ragged; a series of agonizing sounding gasps as he moves within me. He stills, his face contorting as he comes inside of me, liquid heat pulsing into me.

He moans my name as his cock goes wild inside of me, twitching and spurting. He gasps in a breath and then his rigid body relaxes and he slips out of me. He kisses my lips, a gentle graze of a kiss and then he sits back up on his knees. I sit up too and we shuffle around until we're sitting with Aidan's back against the couch back, me leaning on his chest, wrapped in his arms.

He kisses my neck gently.

"Well that was way better than ice cream right?" he says.

I laugh and nod my head.

"Damned right it was. But there's one problem," I say.

"What's that?" Aidan asks, a note of concern in his voice.

"If we had had ice cream instead, we might not have missed the movie," I grin.

Aidan laughs and shakes his head.

"There are plenty of other movies," he says.

"You're right," I say. I twist slightly in his arms so that I can look up at him. "I think we still have time to miss one more tonight."

ERIKA

Last night was every bit as amazing as I had hoped it would be. Aidan and I never even made it as far as the bedroom. We had sex twice on his couch and then we sat up talking in each other's arms for hours. I didn't realize how late (or perhaps I should say early) it had gotten until Aidan's work alarm went off. That's when we realized we had literally been up talking for most of the night.

I had a nice nap this morning. I guess there's one advantage to being on sick leave from work. I can have late nights and then nap the next day. I feel kind of bad for Aidan having to go and do a twelve hour shift on no sleep, but he assured me he's used to it from his intern days when he used to work forty-eight hour shifts most weeks.

I check the time. It's barely one o'clock and Aidan doesn't finish work until six o'clock. I'm meeting him after work, but six o'clock is a long way away. I really need to find myself a hobby or something to do to fill in the hours where I would normally be at work or I'm going to drive myself crazy just sitting around clock watching all day every day. I can't even read – I find myself not focusing on the words, reading them, but not paying attention to them – because all I can think about is Aidan.

My phone starts to ring and I smile to myself as I look for it. One of my friends must have the day off work too. Maybe I can persuade them to go out and do something. Or knowing my luck, it'll be a damned sales call. I finally spot my phone tucked beneath a cushion. I grab it and look at the screen. Jeremy's name is displayed and I feel a moment of apprehension. I hope the constant calls and texts aren't going to start again.

I debate ignoring the call, but I remind myself Jeremy was perfectly normal when I saw him the other day and that maybe he just wants to check in and see if I'm ok. Besides, I'm bored and I'm curious as to what he might want. If he starts with the incessant calls and texts again, I can always go back to ignoring them until he gets the hint again.

"Hello," I say after I press the answer button that flashes green on my screen.

"Hey Erika. I'm not disturbing you am I?" Jeremy says.

Ok so far so good.

"Not at all," I say. "In fact, you're relieving me of my boredom."

Jeremy laughs softly.

"Well that answers my next question which was going to be if you're busy. I got an unexpected day off work and I wondered if you fancied meeting up for lunch?"

"I've already eaten," I lie.

"Coffee then?" Jeremy says.

I hesitate. I don't want to jump to conclusions, but this feels awfully like Jeremy is starting up with the wanting to get back with me thing again.

"Just as friends," he adds.

"I'm not sure it would be a good idea," I say finally.

"Oh come on Erika. It's a cup of coffee not a week in Hawaii," he laughs. "And you've just said yourself that you're bored."

What the hell did I tell him that for?

"Oh what the hell. Why not?" I say.

He's right. I did say I was bored and grabbing some coffee will pass some time until I can see Aidan again. I kind of wish I hadn't lied about already having lunch now as I'm starting to feel hungry and it might have been nice to grab a sandwich or something. I decide I'll have a piece of cake with my coffee and call that lunch.

"Great," Jeremy says. "Do you want me to pick you up or do you want to meet me at Louisa's in half an hour?"

"I'll meet you there," I say.

"Cool. See you in half an hour," Jeremy says and then he ends the call.

I sit in place for a moment wondering if this is really a good idea. I tell myself I'm over thinking it. It's a cup of coffee with friend. And if Jeremy does try to talk me into getting back with him, I can tell him no like I have done a hundred times. We're going to be in a public place, it's not like he's going to beg or anything. And he made it clear we're only going out as friends, so it's not like he can later claim that I was somehow leading him on.

I go to my room and put some sneakers on and grab my jacket and then I head back to the living room, grab my phone and drop it into my hand bag. If I leave now, I'll likely be a little bit early, but I decide I'd rather be early than be stuck sitting here on my own, bored and clock watching, for another minute.

I walk slowly to Louisa's and by the time I get there, I'm only about five minutes early. I'm starting to wonder if I should have said no to this. Jeremy and I always used to come to Louisa's for coffee together before work when we were together and it feels weird being back here now. I debate just leaving and texting him to say something came up, but before I can do it, I hear him calling my name.

I turn around and force myself to smile when I see Jeremy heading towards me.

"Hey," he says. "Have you been here long?"

"No. I just got here," I say.

"In or out?" Jeremy asks, nodding in the direction of the café.

"Out," I say.

It's a nice day and I quite like the idea of getting a bit more fresh air. Jeremy nods and leads me to an empty table. We sit down and within minutes a waitress appears with two menus.

"Just a black coffee and a slice of vanilla sponge cake for me," I say rather than taking the menu.

"And a white coffee for me please," Jeremy adds.

The waitress nods and disappears into the café.

"So how much is it bothering you not going to work then?" Jeremy asks me with a grin.

"A lot," I admit. "Honestly, I would have signed myself off sick leave and went back now, but I think my neck would terrify the kids."

"It doesn't look as bad as you probably think it does," Jeremy says. "But if your doctor gave you a note, there must be a better reason for it than what your bruises look like. Take advantage of the time. Read the classics or something."

That's probably not the worst idea in the world and I nod my head.

"I just might do that," I say.

Except I won't be able to concentrate on them for thinking of Aidan. Something I decide against saying out loud.

Our waitress comes back with our coffees and my cake and as I begin to eat the cake, I realize I'm relaxing. Jeremy isn't being weird and it's starting to feel like we really are just two old friends catching up.

"Do you remember Melanie James?" Jeremy asks me, changing the subject somewhat. The name rings a bell and I try to conjure up a face or a context for it. "She's short. Black hair. Always really intense. Kind of haughty. You used to say she'd …"

"Been a cat in her past life," we finish up together as I finally remember Melanie.

She was a friend Jeremy had introduced me to when we first started dating. I think I've only met her twice, but she is the sort of girl that leaves an impression.

"Didn't she go travelling?" I ask.

"She did, but she's back now. And she brought back quite the souvenir," Jeremy says grinning.

"Come on then, don't keep me in suspense," I laugh.

"She came back married. To a Japanese guy who doesn't speak a word of English. She doesn't speak a word of Japanese. She claims their souls talk to each other," Jeremy said.

I shake my head. I mean who would marry someone they couldn't even talk to? I'm a big believer in love being able to conquer pretty much anything, but how can you love someone when you can't even talk to them? They know literally nothing about each other.

"Crazy huh?" Jeremy says.

"Totally," I agree. "But you said Melanie always was a bit weird so I guess it makes sense for her."

"True," Jeremy smiles. "In some ways, I kind of admire her."

"You do?" I say, surprised.

He nods his head and sips his coffee thoughtfully for a moment and then he puts the cup down and looks at me through the haze of steam rising from the coffee.

"Yeah. I kind of like the way she followed her heart. I mean her head must have been saying that it was likely a mistake, but she didn't listen. Instead, she went with what felt right."

I consider this, but I still can't bring myself to think what she did was a good idea.

"Sometimes though, your head tells you something is a mistake for a reason," I say.

"Oh I'm not saying she hasn't made a mistake. But who knows. Maybe she hasn't. I just think sometimes you need to take a chance. Especially when it comes to love," Jeremy says.

I nod my head. He's probably right about that. I mean look at me and Aidan. We met when I was at my lowest point, and he still took a chance on me.

"That's why I have to say this Erika. I miss you. Every day I miss you. And I want you back," Jeremy says.

Dammit. I really thought this was going well. As in I thought he really had realized we were better off together as friends. It seems he was just leading me into a false sense of security so that he could drop this bombshell on my head.

"Jeremy ..." I start, but he cuts me off and keeps on talking.

"Just think about it Erika. I know we might not have been perfect together, but you can't deny we were good for a while. And I promise I'll try harder this time. Just tell me what you need me to change and I'll change it," he says.

"I don't want you to change anything. I just need you to accept that I don't want to get back with you," I say as gently as I can manage.

"But what about taking a chance on love?" Jeremy says.

I'm going to have to tell him the truth. Maybe then he'll see that this really isn't going to happen and that I've moved on. And once he sees that, then he'll have to see that he has no choice but to move on from this idea of us being together too.

"That's the thing. I am taking a chance on love," I say. "Aidan, who you met outside of the apartment building? We're kind of seeing each other."

"You're seeing Aidan?" Jeremy says.

He doesn't shout. In fact, his voice is so low it's almost a whisper, but I can hear the venom in those words and when he looks at me, his face is a mask of rage. His eyes bore into mine and I feel my stomach turn over.

He clears his throat and blinks and the look is gone, replaced by a look of sad resignation. I wonder if I imagined the look, but I know I didn't. For a second there, the look on Jeremy's face was terrifying. I know I have to finish my coffee quickly and get away from him, and after that, I'm going to go back to ignoring any calls or texts.

This was a mistake and I see it now. I can't help but notice the irony that I took a chance on my head being wrong about this and look where that got me.

"I'm sorry. I didn't know," Jeremy says. He smiles at me. The smile is normal but somehow, it doesn't quite reach his eyes. "I wouldn't have thought he was your type."

Right, because handsome, successful, nice body, funny and kind is so not my type.

"I should have told you sooner. I'm sorry. But it's very new and to be honest, I believed you when you said you only wanted us to be friends so I didn't think it mattered whether you knew or not at this point," I say.

He seems to perk up at that and this time, his smile does reach his eyes. He shakes his head.

"You don't need to apologise. I should be the one apologising. I genuinely did want us to be friends. I thought I was over you, but when I see your smile, hear your laugh, it reminds me that actually, I'm really not over you. But I will get there. I'm not going to start acting like some saddo who hangs around waiting for you to change your mind."

"Maybe it's best if we don't see each other for a while," I say.

I think I see that flicker of anger again, but this time, it's gone so quickly I really think I did imagine it.

"Yeah. Perhaps it is," Jeremy agrees quietly.

Ok, this was awkward, but it wasn't as bad as it could have been. Maybe this is finally the closure Jeremy needs to really move on. Now he knows I'm into Aidan, surely he knows for sure there's no chance for us.

He signals to our waitress and asks for the cheque. It's become kind of awkward between us now and we sit in silence trying not to look at each other as we wait for her to come back. After a few moments, she comes back and places the bill on the table. We both reach for it, but I get it first. Jeremy shakes his head and holds his hand out.

"Come on Erika. I invited you here and put myself out there and you crushed my heart," Jeremy says. He smiles like he's joking, but his eyes say he isn't. "At least let me keep a little dignity and buy your coffee."

I sigh and hand over the bill. I'm not going to argue with him for the price of a cup of coffee and a slice of cake. Jeremy smiles as he takes it. He looks at it and drops some money down with it and we both stand up.

"Well … ummm … I'll see you around then I guess," I say as we move to the front of the café.

Jeremy nods.

"Yeah. See you around. And Erika? What I said before? I still mean it. If you need anything, call me. And if you change your mind about us, well, you know where I am," he says.

I just nod my head. I won't change my mind, but I don't want to rub salt into his wounds so I'll leave that part unsaid.

"Bye," I say and then I turn and walk away, heading back towards the apartment before Jeremy can say anything else.

I reach the end of the block and glance back. A shiver goes through me when I see Jeremy still standing outside of the café, watching me as I walk away. I suddenly feel nervous and I pull my phone out of my pocket. I need to talk to someone as I walk home just to keep me from panicking.

I know I'm over reacting. It's not like Jeremy was following me or anything. He was just watching me walk away, but I keep seeing that flash of anger on his face in the café and even the thought of him watching me walk away makes me feel unsettled.

I scroll through my contacts and find Jennifer's number. It rings for ages and I'm just about to give up when she finally answers.

"Hey Erika. Sorry it took so long to answer. I couldn't find my phone. It was down the back of the damned couch," she says.

"The joys of motherhood," I laugh.

"Yup," she agrees. "So what's up? You sound weird."

I swear Jennifer knows me better than I know myself. I really thought my laughter and our standard joke about the joys of motherhood would cover the fact I was on edge. I wasn't going to tell her what had just happened, I was just going to chat, but now I find myself wanting to tell her. I want to hear her opinion on it, and when she tells me I'm being paranoid and Jeremy is harmless, I know I'll feel better.

"I went for a coffee with Jeremy," I start.

"Oh Erika no," Jennifer says.

"Just as friends," I add quickly. "Or at least that's what I thought it was. He told me he wants us to get back together."

"You're not actually considering it are you?" Jennifer asks. "What about the hot doctor?"

"Of course I'm not considering it. I ended it for a reason with Jeremy and nothing has changed. Besides, I'm so into Aidan. I can't stop thinking about him." I tail off for a moment as Aidan's face swims in front of my mind's eye for a moment. I catch myself and get back on topic. "For a second, when I told Jeremy about Aidan, there was this look on his face. Like not just anger. Actual rage. It was only there for a moment and I might have imagined it I guess, but I was terrified. And then as I walked away from him, he just stood there watching me and I was a bit unnerved so I thought I'd call you."

I didn't really mean to say that much, but once I started talking, it all just kind of tumbled out.

"He's bad news Erika," Jennifer says. "He always has been. It just took you a while to see it."

I frown. I don't know that I've decided Jeremy is bad news. I just don't feel particularly attracted to him. And I had no idea Jennifer felt that way.

"I thought you liked him," I say.

"I did at first," Jennifer admits. "But then he started to isolate you from your friends. At first I thought it was just that rush of lust you have at the beginning of a relationship where you want to be with the person all the time, but then I started to put it together and I realized it was Jeremy who was keeping you away. But he was clever about it. I think he was anyway. I mean he never came out and said you couldn't see your friends or go somewhere right?"

"Right," I say.

I'm about to go on and tell Jennifer she's gotten it all wrong. Jeremy was never a bad guy, he just wasn't for me. She's already talking again though.

"No, instead he would pretend he had planned a surprise for you and guilt trip you into staying home, and then your surprise ended up being something terrible like takeout and it was obvious it wasn't anything Jeremy had planned. He was just manipulating you into being with him and only him."

Is she right or is she just being cynical? I can't decide. I mean Jeremy did have a habit of doing what she was saying he did, but he never pressured me to stay in. I mean he would even tell me that he had planned something but it wasn't important and I should go out. I thought at the time that was so

143

sweet and he really meant it, but now, I wonder if it was all part of the manipulation and I can't help but wonder what his reaction would have been if one time I had said yes, I would still go out.

"Erika? You're not upset with me are you? I'm just telling you how I saw it that's all," Jennifer says.

I realize I've been quiet for too long.

"No. I'm not upset," I say. "I was just thinking. I always just took Jeremy at face value. I never pegged him as a manipulator. I'm still not sure I do."

"That's what made him so good at it. The fact no one would have suspected such a thing of him."

"Hmm," I say, still not totally convinced.

"Look it doesn't matter," Jennifer says. "But if you're serious about Aidan, you can't have Jeremy in your life potentially ruining things for you two. Just promise me you'll stay away from Jeremy for that reason if nothing else."

That I can do.

"Oh I will," I say. "I've told him there's no chance of getting back together and I'm going to go back to just ignoring the phone if he calls or anything again."

"Good," Jennifer says.

I hear a beeping sound in my ear and I pull the phone away for a second to look at the screen. Aidan is trying to get through.

"Jennifer?" I say, bringing the phone back to my ear. "Aidan is on the other line. Can ..."

"Just go," Jennifer laughs. "Take his call and forget all about Jeremy."

She hangs up and I press answer on Aidan's call.

"Hi," I say.

"Hey," he says.

He doesn't sound happy to be talking to me. In fact, he sounds pissed off.

"What's wrong?" I ask.

"Something came up," he says. "One of the doctors called in sick and I'm going to have to work late tonight. I'm really sorry but I'm going to have to cancel dinner."

I feel myself deflating. I was really looking forward to seeing Aidan again tonight and going back to his place once he had finished work. It can't be helped though. It's not like he has the sort of job where he can just walk out when his shift is done. His job is life and death, and if he has to work late, he has to work late.

"Ok," I say. "Maybe tomorrow instead?"

"You're not mad?" Aidan asks, sounding surprised.

"No of course not. I mean I'm disappointed, but I get it," I say.

"Tomorrow it is then. And I'll make tonight up to you," he says.

"Now that sounds like a plan," I say.

We chat for a few minutes and then Aidan has to go. By the time we're done, I'm almost back at the apartment. I think for a moment and I come up with a plan. I turn around and walk back the way I have just come, heading for the store on the corner.

I go inside and buy a cooked chicken, some fresh bread, some ingredients for a salad and a small cheesecake. I pay and leave the store heading back to the apartment again.

If Aidan can't come to dinner, then dinner will have to go to Aidan. I know he'll be busy, but he must get a break, and when he does, I'll be waiting and we'll have a little romantic picnic in the break room.

I smile to myself as I go into the apartment and head to the kitchen to start preparing some chicken sandwiches and salads. Maybe it'll be quiet enough that we might get to fool around after the picnic. God I hope so. I crave Aidan's touch so much. I really don't think I can wait until tomorrow to have him in my arms again.

AIDAN

I can't believe I have had to call Erika and cancel tonight. I was really looking forward to seeing her and I'm gutted I won't be able to now. I'm also gutted that I've let her down already and it would have only been our second official date. She seemed to understand though which is something I guess. Still though, as six o'clock comes and goes and I know I should have been on my way to meet Erika outside of the hospital now, but instead am stuck at work, I feel a pang of regret.

I'm starting to think about what I can do tomorrow night to make tonight up to Erika when there's a knock on my office door.

"Come in," I call.

The door opens and Stacy limps in.

"What happened?" I ask, getting up to help her keep the weight off her foot.

147

"I slipped in the hall and fell. I think it's just twisted, but would you mind taking a quick look at it?" she replies as I guide her into a chair.

"Sure," I say. "No problem."

I kneel down in front of her. She slips her shoe off and I gently begin to feel around her ankle. She winces slightly.

"Sorry," I say.

"It's ok," she smiles. "For a nurse, I'm surprisingly bad with pain."

"I think most of us are," I laugh.

I keep feeling around her ankle. Nothing feels out of place and I move on to her actual foot, feeling over the top and bottom of it and around her heel. She giggles as I touch the bottom of her foot.

"That tickles," she says.

She flexes her toes as I feel around her foot, rubbing them on my hand and I have a feeling it's intentional.

"You know," Stacy says, her voice light and amused. "I normally make a guy buy me dinner before he gets to feel me up like this."

Oh the touch was intentional alright. I know Stacy is just making a joke though and it's harmless, and so I play along, not really flirting back, but keeping the joke going.

"If you let guys feel you up like this, you're doing it wrong," I smile.

"Oh. And how should they be doing it?" Stacy says.

I glance up at her. She twirls a strand of hair around her finger and smiles down at me. I resist the urge to roll my eyes.

"I'm sure you can figure it out," I say. I get to my feet, noting the look of disappointment on Stacy's face. "Nothing's broken. It's just a light sprain. Let me grab a bandage and once we get your foot bandaged up, you'll barely feel it."

"Thanks," she says.

I move over to a cabinet filled with supplies and grab a long ace bandage and a clip to fasten the bandage with. I move back to Stacy and kneel down between her knees again. A knock sounds on my door as I reach for Stacy's foot.

"Come in," I call.

I see Stacy's expression change as the door opens. She isn't pleased that we're being interrupted. I peer around Stacy and smile with delight when I see Erika coming into my office.

"Oh I'm sorry. Am I interrupting something?" she says. "Your secretary said it was ok to come in."

"No, its fine," I tell her. "Come on in and grab a seat. I won't be long. Stacy slipped and hurt her ankle in the hallway. I'm just bandaging it up for her."

Erika moves closer to us and sits down behind my desk. She doesn't look in the least bit impressed to find me on the ground between Stacy's legs with her bare foot in my hand. Stacy looks equally unimpressed at having Erika join us. Somehow, I've gone from bandaging a foot to having both of these women pissed off at me for no real reason.

Stacy glances at Erika and her eyes widen for a second.

"I know you. You were a patient here weren't you?" she says. "You were attacked in your home right?"

Erika nods her head. I would have preferred to keep this quiet around the hospital for a little longer, but technically, I'm doing nothing wrong and I'm so happy to see Erika here right now that I no longer care who knows about us.

"Dr Miller. Fraternising with your patients. How naughty," Stacy says with fake shock.

"She isn't my patient now," I point out. "Nothing happened between us until after she had been discharged."

"A likely story," Stacy jokes. I open my mouth to tell her I'm being serious, but she goes on before I can. "So now you're picking women up from the wards, I'll have to keep an eye on bed nineteen. She's pretty cute."

Erika's cheeks are beaming red and I feel pretty uncomfortable myself. I wrap the bandage more quickly, trying to just get it done and get Stacy away from my office before she manages to convince Erika I make a habit of dating my patients.

Stacy turns to Erika and winks at her.

"You know, I always thought Aidan only had eyes for me," she says.

She laughs as she says it, but the laugh doesn't sound entirely real. Erika gives a fake sounding laugh too. Its clear Stacy is making Erika feel uncomfortable and I have no idea what to say that won't just make it worse so I keep quiet. I attach the fastener to the bandage and get up, practically jumping away from Stacy.

"All done," I say.

Stacy pushes her foot back into her shoe and stands up. She gingerly tests her bad foot on the ground. She makes a moaning sound that wouldn't be out of place in the bedroom and smiles at me.

"Thanks doc, that feels great," she smiles.

"It's just a bandage," I say awkwardly.

"Oh come on, we both know it's more than that," she purrs.

"Huh?" I say, thrown completely by her statement.

I barely dare look at Erika but I risk a quick glance at her. She's bright red, staring down into her lap. I don't know if she's upset or angry, but either way, I just want Stacy gone so I can try and salvage this situation.

Stacy giggles at my discomfort. She moves closer to me and bumps my hip with hers.

"You have magic hands," she grins.

I laugh awkwardly and shuffle away from her.

"Well I'd better get back on the ward," Stacy says. I feel myself relaxing slightly as she heads for the door. She pulls it open and turns back to me. "When we go for that drink, the first round is on me. As a thank you for fixing my foot."

She slips away before I can say anything, pulling the door shut behind her. I turn to Erika who finally looks up at me.

"Well that was awkward," I say, trying and failing to remove some of the tension I can see written all over Erika.

"Yes," she agrees. "I should go. I'm clearly interrupting something."

She stands up and I move around the desk, blocking her escape route.

"You're not interrupting anything," I say. "Stacy slipped and hurt her ankle that's all."

"Right," Erika says. "And the flirting? I just imagined that?"

"No," I admit. "But that's just Stacy. It doesn't mean anything Erika."

"You're going on a date with her," Erika says. "That means it means something."

I smile. I can't help it. The idea of me choosing Stacy over Erika is the craziest thing I've heard in years, and I have to admit that I find her jealousy a little bit endearing. It's good to know she would care if she thought I was going out with Stacy.

"Not in a million years," I say. "Stacy asked me if I wanted to grab a drink after work the other night. I said no and she said some other time. I said sure to that because I didn't want to hurt her feelings. But it's not going to happen. And even if it did, it wouldn't be a date. It would be colleagues grabbing a quick drink together."

"I'm not sure that's the way she'd see it," Erika comments.

I shrug.

"Who cares what anyone else thinks? As long as we know the truth," I say.

I move closer to her and pull her into my arms. She resists my embrace ever so slightly at first and then she relents and softens against me, wrapping her arms around my waist. I kiss the top of her head.

"I swear to you Erika, I'm not into Stacy. Or anyone else for that matter. I know it's a bit soon to say this, but I really like you and I don't want to even think about dating anyone else right now," I say.

She keeps her arms around me but she pulls her head back so she can look up at me.

"Right answer," she smiles.

I lean down and kiss her, this time on the lips. Instantly fire floods my body and I can feel my cock responding to the taste of Erika's mouth. I want nothing more than to swipe the desk clean, throw Erika on top of it, and make love to her. I resist the urge. The place is busy and there's always a chance I'll be needed and someone will come to grab me. Not only would it be embarrassing if they caught me and Erika fucking, it could also slow my reaction down enough to cost a life in an emergency situation.

With that in mind, I gently pull my lips away from Erika's. Her eyes open and she peers at me with a smile.

"Probably a good job you stopped that," she says. "Or I would have had no choice but to ride you on the floor right there."

I moan as a wave of longing goes through me. Erika giggles and steps out of my arms.

"Do you have a spare half hour or so?" she asks.

"Erika, we can't," I say. "As much as I'd like to, I'm on call and if anyone comes in …"

I trail off when I see the amusement on her face.

"I meant for dinner," she laughs. She points to a bag on the ground that I didn't notice when she came in. "I know you had to miss our special dinner, so I thought I'd bring dinner to you, picnic style."

"I can spare a half hour," I confirm. "But if there's an emergency, I might have to run out without any warning."

"Yeah obviously I'm not suggesting you should let someone die so we can eat together," Erika smiles.

She picks up the bag and begins to pull the food out of it. She pulls out a blanket which she spreads on my office floor and then she arranges the food and sits down on the blanket, patting the ground beside her. I sit down and we start to eat.

"The stars are beautiful this evening," I grin, tilting my head back and looking up at the ceiling.

Erika laughs and shakes her head.

"What?" I say. "I'm just getting into the picnic spirit."

"You think this was a stupid idea don't you?" she says.

"No," I say quickly, shaking my head. "I don't think that at all. In fact, I think it's a great idea."

"You do?" she asks.

I nod my head.

"I really do," I say. "It's very romantic and in some ways it's better than a real picnic. There's no rain, no bugs, no wind. It's perfect."

She smiles and leans in for a kiss. I oblige her and instantly, I want to strip her off and make love to her again. She pulls away first this time and laughs softly.

"We have to stop doing that," she says.

"I never want to stop doing that," I tell her. "But I know what you mean. Ok, before we can get any further. Tell me about your day."

"I went for a coffee with Jeremy," Erika says.

Ok, that did it. Mentioning Jeremy is a great mood killer. I instantly feel a mix of insane jealousy at the thought of Jeremy getting to spend time with Erika and a feeling of trepidation at the thought of her being around someone I think might be dangerous.

"It was a mistake," Erika adds quickly.

"How so?" I ask.

She looks down at her lap for a moment and shakes her head.

"I thought he really meant it when he said he had accepted we were better as friends. It turns out I was wrong. He told me he missed me and he wanted us to get back together," she says.

"And what did you tell him?" I ask.

Erika looks at me, a teasing smile on her face.

"I told him we should get married and have a hundred babies," she says with a laugh. I raise an eyebrow and she laughs again. "I told him no obviously. I told him I was into you. I hope that's ok."

"Of course it's ok. It's better than ok," I say, unable to keep the goofy grin from my face. "How did he take it?"

"I'm not sure," Erika says. "For a second, he gave me this look and it was filled with such intense rage that I felt cold inside. Like I was scared of him for a moment. But then the look was gone and he was really apologetic and back to acting normal. I keep trying to convince myself that I only imagined the look, but I really don't think I did."

I don't think she did either. I think Jeremy is a grade A psychopath that won't rest until he has Erika back where he wants her. I keep that opinion to myself. I don't want to worry Erika and I don't want her to think my jealousy is clouding my judgement. If she thinks that, then she might stop telling me things like this, and if Jeremy continues sniffing around her, I want to know about it.

"I get where he's coming from," I say, trying to keep my tone light. "I'd be pretty bummed to lose you too."

Erika smiles at me and bites her bottom lip.

"There's not much chance of that happening," she says. She's quiet for a moment and then she speaks again. "Jennifer, my best friend, admitted she never really liked Jeremy. She said he was manipulative and emotionally blackmailed me into staying away from my friends. She thinks I should stay away from him."

"I'm probably a little bit biased here, but I think you should stay away from him too," I say. She grins and I laugh softly. "Seriously though, if your best friend thought there was something off about him, it might be a good idea to give him a wide berth for a while."

"I'm going to," Erika says. "If he calls or texts or anything, I'm just going to ignore him. I tried to be nice and stay friends with him and that clearly didn't work."

I nod, satisfied that at least Erika isn't going to walk into another situation with Jeremy. I'm not convinced he won't keep trying to run into her though. My mind flashes to the car that was parked outside of her building the other night. I am finding it harder and harder to convince myself that wasn't Jeremy.

"So how's your day been? Other than flirting with the nurses?" Erika asks.

"Busy but boring," I say. "Just the same emergency room stuff."

We finish eating as I tell Erika about my boring day. There's really nothing to tell, but she seems interested in how it all works and so I tell her. I collect our trash as I talk and put it in my trash can and Erika folds the blanket back up and puts it back in her bag.

"Is your break over then?" she asks.

I open my mouth to tell her I can take another ten minutes. My rounds are done and it's mostly paperwork I have to do now and that can wait. I'm really only here in case I'm needed now. A knock comes on my door before I can say anything and I realize even thinking I can take a few extra minutes to myself has most likely jinxed me.

"Come in," I call.

Julia steps into my office. She smiles at Erika and then me.

"I'm sorry to interrupt Aidan, but Mr Warburton in bed seven is having some pain. He's had his maximum dose of painkillers and I wondered if you could take a look and see if there's anything we can do for him. He's getting quite distressed."

"Of course," I say.

Erika has already gathered her things.

"I guess that's my cue to leave," she smiles.

"Sorry," Julia says again.

"It's fine," I tell her. "I'll be right there."

Julia nods and backs out of my office. I know Julia is experienced enough that she would recognize someone attention seeking or being a bit dramatic. If she says Mr Warburton is in pain, then he is, and I don't want to make him wait to be seen. I also don't want to leave Erika either.

"Go," Erika smiles at me. "I'll see you tomorrow."

I kiss her quickly, a barely there kiss because I can't afford to be distracted now. I rush from my office and I hear Erika leaving behind me. I can't help but glance back and watch her ass as she walks away.

AIDAN

I t's almost midnight when I'm finally ready to leave the hospital. It's been a long day and I'm ready to go home, crawl into bed, and try to get some sleep. At least with working over today, I have a slightly later start tomorrow. I don't have to come in until eight instead of five so I might actually have a chance to sleep in in the morning. Last night with Erika was well worth feeling tired for today, but it's starting to take its toll now.

I pull on my jacket and lock my office door, heading back through the ward. I say goodnight to the nurses I pass and a couple of insomniac patients who wander the corridors going back and forth to the bathroom or chatting to the nurses to pass the time. I manage to escape the ward without being stopped, but it's not until I step out of the doors and take in a deep breath of the chilly night air that I actually allow myself to breathe a sigh of relief. I learned my lesson about jinxing myself earlier when I opened my mouth to tell Erika I could take a little bit more time.

I head towards the staff parking lot. Even at this time, it's pretty full. Although the outpatient clinics are long closed for the night, the wards all need to be staffed and the emergency room is fully staffed too. For that reason, I'm not overly surprised to see someone else in the car park. There's always people coming and going here. I am however surprised when I realise he's sitting on the hood of my car.

I frown and pick up my pace, wondering what's going on. It's likely a mistake – someone waiting for one of the staff members to finish work and thinking this is their car. The guy is likely going to be pretty embarrassed when I walk up and he realizes his mistake.

As I get closer though, I realize I'm the one who has made the mistake. The man sitting on my car hood is Jeremy. And he's clearly there waiting for me. I feel my body tense up, ready for a fight. I am not in the mood for Jeremy right now, and although I'm not an advocate for brawling in the street, I know it won't take much to push me into a fight tonight.

"Can I help you?" I demand when I am close enough to the car to be able to speak without yelling.

I expect Jeremy to jump at the sound of my voice cutting through the still night air, but he doesn't. He pushes himself casually off the car hood and turns to face me. He smiles at me, a cold smile that I don't like one little bit.

"Yes, you can help me," he says. "You can stay the hell away from Erika."

I shake my head as I walk towards the driver's side door of the car.

"Yeah that's not going to happen. So why don't you run along back to wherever the hell you came from and stay out of Erika's life," I say.

Jeremy looks at me like he's a little surprised that I didn't immediately agree to do his bidding. Just how delusional is this guy?

"You don't get it do you?" he says. "Erika is mine. She has always been mine and she always will be mine. I've done the right thing. I've warned you. And if you choose not to heed that warning, then believe me when I say that there will be consequences."

I've heard enough. I gave him a chance to just walk away but he's still here pushing me. I walk away from my car door and move around to the front of the car to meet Jeremy face to face.

"Listen here," I say. "I don't appreciate being threatened and I don't appreciate you hanging around Erika when she's made it clear to you that you two are over. And if I find out that you've hurt her in any way, then I swear I'll make you fucking sorry."

"Is everything ok here?" a voice asks from behind me before Jeremy can respond to me.

I turn to look and see a security guard approaching us. As if by some unspoken agreement, Jeremy and I each take a step back from each other.

"Everything's fine," I say.

"Yup, all good," Jeremy says, still backing away from me, his hands raised showing his palms. "Stay away from my girl Aidan."

The last part is said over his shoulder as he walks briskly across the parking lot away from me. I shake my head. The security guard comes closer.

"What was all of that about?" he asks.

"Oh it was nothing. Just some jerk that has nothing better to do with his time than try to threaten me," I say.

"Should I call the police?" the security guard asks.

"No," I say. "It's nothing I can't handle."

"Well if you're sure …?" the security guard says.

"I am," I assure him. "Goodnight."

"Night," he says.

He wanders away to go back to his perimeter rounds and I get into my car. I half wish I had let the security guard call the police. It might have put Jeremy on their radar. But the chances of the responding officers being Officer Prescott and Officer Moore would have been unlikely at best. And what was I supposed to tell the police? Jeremy was mean to me? No, it would have been too embarrassing. Especially if Erika had found out about it. It would have either looked like I was a crazy guy who was making trouble for Jeremy just because I was jealous, or it would have looked like I was scared of him. Neither of those were good looks.

I sigh as I put my car into reverse and pull out of the parking lot. I start heading for home, but then I change my mind. I might not be scared of Jeremy hurting me, but I am becoming more and more convinced that it was him that had attacked Erika, and I am definitely scared that he will try to hurt her again if she keeps rejecting his advances. He doesn't seem like the sort of guy who gives up easily and that's not good for Erika.

Now he knows where Erika is staying, I really didn't like the thought of her and Nadia being alone in the apartment if Jeremy should show up. I make a U-turn and head for Nadia's place. It's late and I figure Nadia and Erika will likely already be in bed, but I have a key to the apartment so I can just let myself in and crash on the couch.

In the morning when I am discovered, I will just say I was too tired to drive all the way home. Nadia is used to finding me crashed on her couch after a long shift at the hospital as her place is closer to it, and so she won't think it's too weird. And Erika will have no reason to not believe my story when Nadia confirms I often do this.

By the time I arrive at Nadia's place and let myself in and go to lay down on the couch, I'm starting to debate whether or not I should just come clean about the whole Jeremy thing. I really should warn Erika. But I already know what she'll say. She'll say he's harmless and to just ignore him, that he's just pissed off. And there's a chance that she'll confront him about it, and that will only put her in the line of more danger. No, for now, I'm going to keep this to myself until I can prove for sure that Jeremy is dangerous. And now I don't dare tell Nadia, because chances are she'll let it slip to Erika and then Erika will be pissed off with me for going behind her back and keeping this from her.

I lay in the darkness, trying to push all of the thoughts about Jeremy out of my mind. It's funny, but now I'm here laying down in the darkness, the idea of sleeping is far from my mind. All I can think about is that just two doors from where

I am laying now, Erika is lying in bed. And I want so badly to go to her.

My cock is hard at the thought of me getting up and going and slipping into bed with her. I want to do it so badly, and I know that until I do, I'm not going to get any sleep tonight. I wonder if it's too forward. I don't think it is. Erika was as frustrated as me earlier about us not being able to do more than kiss. I think she'll be happy to see me, and if she's not, I will just apologize for over stepping the line and come back out here. I have to try it though. If I don't and later find out Erika would have welcomed my visit, I will absolutely kick myself.

Quietly, I open the door leading to the bedrooms and creep into the hallway. I tap on Erika's bedroom door but there's no answer. I push the door open and go into the room. I stand for a moment looking at her. She is asleep, her mouth slightly open, her face peaceful looking. A silver flash of moonlight lights her up, making her look radiant. Her hair is fanned out on the pillow beside her. It's so shiny it looks wet. I smile as I watch her for a moment.

She is really gorgeous and I can't wait another moment to be in the bed beside her. I slowly and quietly strip off my clothes and make my way to Erika's bed. She stirs as I lift the sheet and slip in beside her.

ERIKA

I come awake slowly as the mattress dips beside me. My heart slams in my chest and I come fully awake instantly, my eyes flying open. Who the fuck is in my room in the middle of the night, getting into my bed with me?

"It's ok, it's just me," a voice says.

"Aidan?" I say. As my eyes adjust to the darkness, I see I'm right. Aidan is in my bed beside me. "What are you doing here?"

"I missed you," he whispers.

He puts his mouth on my shoulder, kissing the bare skin there and I moan, my body instantly coming to life beneath his kisses. I'm still confused. How did Aidan even get in here? His mouth moves to my neck and I realize I don't care how or why he's here. I only care that he is. I mean it is his sister's apartment. He most likely has a key to the place.

I turn so I'm facing him and I scoot closer to him, wrapping my arm around him and pressing my lips against his. I

IONA ROSE

realize as I press myself against him that he's naked. My insides are swirling, desire pumping through me, and feeling Aidan's bare skin against mine only makes me hotter for him. God I'm glad he's here.

I hook my leg over his hip, pushing him onto his back and rolling with him. I sit up straddling him and move my hips so my pussy rubs over his rock hard cock. He moans as I tease him. I lean forward and kiss him, cutting off his moan. Our tongues collide, massaging against each other and sending shivers through my body.

Aidan runs his hands over my bare sides and back, cupping my ass for a moment and then running back up my sides. He moves his hands to the front of my body and begins to work my nipples between his fingers. Bursts of electricity run through my sensitive nipples and down my body, making my clit pulse with need. Aidan moves his mouth from mine and shuffles down the bed beneath me until his head is beneath my breasts. He sucks one of my nipples into his mouth.

The warmth of his lips and the feeling of his rough tongue lapping over my now rock hard nipple send me into a frenzy and I have to bite my lip to stop myself from calling out his name, conscious of Nadia in the other bedroom. Aidan nips my nipple between his teeth and a blast of intense pleasure assaults me. It's so intense it's verging on being painful, and it wakes my body up in ways I have never even imagined were possible.

He releases my nipple from his mouth and I gasp quietly as the cool air replaces his warm lips. Goose bumps flood down my body as Aidan sucks my other nipple into his mouth, and I don't know if it's the cold or his expert licking that makes my body dance with goose bumps. I only know I like it.

Aidan brings me right to the edge of a climax and then he releases my nipple and scoots back up the bed, kissing me hard on the lips. I melt into his kiss, moving my hips now almost instinctively rather than to tease him. I can feel his hard cock rubbing over my clit as I writhe around and my climax explodes through me. I make a moaning sound, muffled by Aidan's kiss as fire floods my body, lighting me up from the inside out.

I have to pull my mouth from his and I press my face against his neck to muffle the sounds coming from me unbidden. I am riding on the waves of pleasure as they crash over me leaving me feeling disorientated and frozen against Aidan's body.

When I feel like I can move again, I run my tongue lightly down Aidan's neck and then over his shoulder and down his chest. I scoot backwards, still running my tongue over his salty tasting skin.

I stop when my mouth reaches Aidan's cock. I grip it in my fist and push my lips over the tip, swirling my tongue over it. Aidan's hands fist up at his sides as I lower my head, taking him right into my mouth. I bob my head, moving my lips and tongue up and down Aidan's length. He moans quietly as I get into a rhythm, working him mercilessly.

I start to move my fist in time with my mouth, my movements getting faster. Aidan's quiet moans spur me on, and I reach up with my other hand and begin to caress his balls. He moans louder. I am so caught up in pleasuring him, that for a moment, I allow myself to forget about Nadia in the other room, forget about being quiet and just lose myself in the moment.

I go to town on Aidan and I feel his cock twitch, the first salty wave of his cum spurting into my mouth. I swallow it, still sucking on him. I am rewarded with another spurt and still I suck, wanting to suck him dry, greedily drinking down his cum.

Finally, I stop and I come up onto my knees. I wipe my mouth on the back of my hand as I look down at Aidan. His eyes are heavy with lust, a sated grin on his face. His hair is mussed up and he looks so sexy that I feel a jolt of electricity flow through me just at the sight of him. His chest is rising and falling quickly as he pants for breath and I watch it for a moment, admiring the defined muscles there.

Aidan pushes himself up onto his elbows, that lazy grin still on his face. I move back up his body and lean down to meet him. Our lips meld together, our kiss passionate and raw, communicating our desperate need for each other without words. Aidan wraps his arms around me and flips me onto my back. He pulls his lips from mine and smiles down at me.

"Your turn," he grins.

He moves downwards across the mattress, scooting between my legs. He leans forward, grasping my inner thighs. He pushes my legs further apart and then he moves flat onto his front, his face pressed into my mound. I gasp as his tongue finds my swollen clit and begins to move. Instantly my body is on the verge of a climax again as Aidan expertly works me, varying the pace between a full on assault of my senses and a slower, more relaxed movement. He seems to sense exactly when to change the pace to keep me right on the edge of an orgasm without letting me go over and fully experience it.

It is both frustrating and delicious and I am floating on a wave of desire and pleasure. He keeps going, and I don't know which way is up. All I know is that I need the release my orgasm will bring me and I need it now. I scoot down a little bit, moving closer to Aidan, pressing myself tightly against his face. I wrap my legs around his shoulders, holding him in place.

His tongue laps me slowly, moving my clit from side to side. I can hardly breathe from the anticipation of the orgasm that's almost upon me. I close my eyes and suck in an almost painful breath as Aidan slows the pace once more.

I can't take this teasing any longer and I tighten my thighs, tightening my hold on Aidan, and I begin to thrust my hips, forcing Aidan to up the pace. He takes my lead and licks my clit fast and hard and even when I stop thrusting, he doesn't slow the pace. I am hurtling towards my orgasm, my body pulsing and tingling, poised and ready for the pleasure to flood through me.

My orgasm slams through me, starting in my clit and my stomach and then spreading out through the rest of my body. I can feel my pussy clenching, warm juices running from it. My clit is pulsing, my stomach is contracting and every part of my body tingles with heat. Still Aidan is working me, keeping me in the throes of my orgasm, not letting me relax and catch my breath for even a second.

I can see red spots dancing in front of my eyes. They flicker in time with the pulses of pleasure going through me. I can't breathe, I can't move. All of my muscles are rigid, holding me in place while my senses are battered, assaulted with deliciousness. The red spots get bigger and I feel my eyes rolling back in my head. For a second, everything goes black and then my eyes fly open, my head spinning deliriously as my body pulses.

Finally, when I don't think I can take anymore, Aidan reaches up and disentangles my legs from his shoulders and moves his face away from me. I lay in place, my heart racing, finally able to breathe again. I suck in a giant lungful of air and the dizziness begins to fade. I keep gasping and panting, trying to come back to myself. I feel like I came undone during my orgasm. I have never felt anything like that before in my life, and even as I recover from it, I'm already craving the moment when I will feel it again.

Aidan crawls back up my body and kisses me. I can taste myself on his lips, on his tongue. I run my hands over the smooth muscles of his back, pressing him tighter against me. Without warning, Aidan pushes his cock inside of me and I gasp as he fills me up once more.

He begins to move his hips, thrusting into me, and my body follows his lead, settling into his rhythm, working with him in perfect tandem. He moves faster, his cock rubbing over my g-spot with each stroke and I can feel another orgasm coming on. I push my hands into Aidan's hair as I come, balling it into my fists and tugging on it as pleasure once more floods through me.

I cry out his name and then I remember myself and bite down on the inside of my bottom lip to keep from crying out again. I can hear myself making a whimpering sound as Aidan pumps into me. He is moving faster now and I feel his body tense up as he hits his orgasm. His body goes stiff, and he moans against my neck as he comes hard once more.

We lay in place for a moment and then Aidan rolls off me and we lay in the darkness, panting for breath.

"Holy fucking shit," I whisper when I trust myself to speak again.

"Yeah I reckon that about sums it up," Aidan grins.

He rolls onto his side and props himself up on one elbow, looking down on me. He leans in and we kiss, a tender kiss this time. He strokes my cheek when he pulls his lips back from mine.

"You're beautiful," he says.

I feel my cheeks flush at his compliment and I just shake my head. He laughs softly.

"Yeah you are," he says.

He kisses me again and then he lays down and I roll onto my side so that I'm facing him. He puts his arm around me and pulls me closer.

"Just so you know," I whisper. "You can cancel dinner anytime if it means we get to do that later."

Aidan laughs softly, his breath warm on my face.

"In that case, I reckon we'll be cancelling breakfast in the morning," he says.

I feel a delicious shiver go through me at his words. I don't know if I can wait until the morning to have him again, but my body is spent and I accept that I don't have the energy to so much as move an inch, let alone do that again right now.

I close my eyes, enjoying the weight of Aidan's arm on my waist, breathing in the scent of him. Laying here like this feels more right than anything I have ever done before in my life and I know that I will never get tired of Aidan, never lose that spark that we have between us, and I know that whatever the future might hold for me, I see Aidan in it.

AIDAN

The alarm on my phone blares out, pulling me out of a dream where Erika and I were getting pretty hot and heavy. I reach out to shut off the alarm but my phone isn't on my bedside table. I sit up, rubbing the sleep out of my eyes and I see I'm not at home. A smile curls over my lips when I remember where I am and what happened last night. I'm at Nadia's place, in Erika's bed. I came here after … No. I'm not going to let memories of my encounter with Jeremy ruin this moment.

I jump out of bed and grab my jeans, taking my phone from the pocket and silencing my alarm. I turn back to the bed and I see I am alone in the room. Erika is gone. I open the bedroom door a crack and listen. I hear water running and I figure Erika must be in the shower. I move back to her bed and slip back beneath the covers. I sit up, my back pressed against the headboard. I know if I let myself lay back down, I'll end up falling asleep again and I have to be at work soon. I don't want to miss my chance to have some time with Erika before I have to leave.

I imagine Erika in the shower, water and soap suds running over her skin. I imagine myself in there with her, running my hands over her slick body, kissing her wet lips. I imagine myself lifting her up, her legs wrapping around my waist, and us fucking hard underneath the shower spray.

I'm hard at the thought of it. I debate going to Erika, but I don't know how she'll feel about the idea with Nadia here so I force myself to stay where I am. I can't stop myself from thinking about how good it would feel though, the heat of the water, the heat of Erika. Her slick wet pussy, her wetness there nothing to do with the shower. I can almost hear her purring my name as her pussy clenches around my cock as she comes hard.

God she came hard last night. I made her body sing, made her feel things I don't think she'd ever felt before. And my God did she do the same for me. She woke parts of my body up that I didn't even know I had. She made me feel like I was flying, soaring through the clouds on a wave of ecstasy. I need to have her. Now.

My cock is so hard it's almost uncomfortable and I'm tempted to reach down and grab it, but I resist the urge. I want to save myself for Erika. I want to be ready to give her a repeat of last night the second she walks back into the room.

I try to think about something else, anything to stop myself from being too eager, but I can't do it. My head is full of Erika. My skin still smells of her. She is consuming me and it feels so damned good. I know we haven't known each for very long, but I already know that I have never felt this way about anyone before. I have never met anyone who consumes both my waking thoughts and my dreams so completely.

A pulse of excitement goes through me when I hear the bathroom door click open. I am almost holding my breath with delicious anticipation as the door handle of the bedroom pushes down and then the door opens and Erika is in the room, a vision of beauty. Her hair is dripping wet, and she's naked except for a fluffy white towel that she's wrapped around herself. She smiles at me when she sees I am awake.

I don't speak. I just push the sheet off me and go to her. I pull the towel away in one swift movement, dropping it to the ground and pulling Erika against me. She doesn't resist me. Her lips seek out mine as insistently as mine seek out hers. I kiss her, a full passionate kiss that sends my cock into overdrive once more. I kiss her for a long time, my hands roaming over her body as hers roam over mine. When I can't take the waiting any longer, I spin her around in my arms, pulling her back against me.

I run my fingers down the front of her body, running them between her breasts and over her flat stomach until I come to her pussy. I push my fingers between her lips and find her clit. She gasps as I press on it, a pained sound, and I ease up the pressure.

"Keep going," she whispers. "I'm just a little tender after last night that's all."

I don't need telling twice once I know I'm not really hurting her. I work her clit, making her gasp again. Her pained gasping sounds turn into gasps of pleasure and I can feel how wet she is. Her juices coat my fingers, leaving them deliciously sticky.

My cock is on fire, and I can hardly breathe in anticipation of sinking into Erika's warm depths. I can't wait any longer. I start to walk forward, moving Erika with me until we're almost at the wall. I put my hands on her shoulders, pushing her forward. She seems to know what I want and she bends at the waist, bracing her palms on the wall.

I run my fingers back through her lips, spreading her wetness around and then I push against her thighs, spreading her legs further open. She is a vision, bent over, her glistening pussy on display. I swallow hard as I push inside of her and begin to thrust. She thrusts with me, pushing herself back onto me with a passionate force that sends shivers running through my body.

I reach around her, teasing one of her nipples between my fingers. My other hand goes back to her clit, my fingers finding it as though I am drawn right to it. I work her as I thrust. I know she's getting close to coming when I feel her body tensing up and hear the little gasping sound her breathing makes.

I slam into her again and her pussy tightens around me, holding me in place for a second. A shudder goes through Erika's whole body as she moans and when her knees give way, I catch her around the waist, stopping her from falling. I pull her upper body back up against my own and step closer to the wall, bracing my palms on it on either side of Erika.

I pump into her until I can't hold back any longer. I come hard, my orgasm screaming through my body, turning my muscles to delicious jelly. I whisper Erika's name against her neck as I come.

I slip out of her and she turns in my arms, clinging to me, breathless. I move backwards, bringing her back to the bed where we both collapse beside each other.

"That was a perfect start to the day," Erika says after a moment. She rolls towards me and lays with her head on my chest. "But there's one problem."

"What's that?" I ask.

I'm not concerned. Her tone is light and joking and I don't think there's really a problem.

"How do we top that? When your day starts that well, it can only go downhill right?" she says.

"I'm not sure that's true," I say.

"Oh really?" Erika says, lifting her head and looking at me with a smile. "So what do you suggest?"

"I suggest you meet me after work tonight and come back to my place with me and I'll show you what comes next," I say. "Let's just call that a warm up."

Erika grins at me and leans in to kiss me.

"I like the sound of that," she says. She pauses and then grins again. "So how long do you have before work? Because I could sure use another warm up right about now."

I check my watch and groan.

"Shit. I have like half an hour," I say. "And in that time I have to shower and get to the hospital."

She moves aside a little reluctantly and I stand up, already missing the warmth of Erika's body against mine.

"Are you sure I can't tempt you to be a little late?" she asks.

"Believe me, I'm tempted, but I really do have to get moving," I say.

I make no move to leave the room. Looking at her laying on the bed, her thighs parted, is too mesmerising to walk away from. She grins at me and runs her fingers up her inner thigh.

"Are you sure?" she asks. "You're not even a tiny bit tempted to stay?"

I moan and climb back onto the bed beside her.

"I'll make my shower super quick," I say as she giggles and grabs me, pulling me down on top of her.

ERIKA

I grab Aidan and pull him down on top of me, giggling at his reluctance to leave me. My giggles are cut short as Aidan's mouth comes down over mine. My lips tingle where they touch his, and I am instantly ready for him once more. I don't think there will ever be a time when I'm not instantly ready for him. He has a way to set my soul on fire just by looking at him, just by being near him. Hell, just by thinking about him. I have never known anything like it and although it scares me a little bit to have fallen for him so quickly, I also love the way he can make me feel.

I don't want him to go, but I know he has to and I know we don't have much time so I don't waste any of the time we do have before I grab his cock. I move my fist up and down it, loving the sound of Aidan's moans as he moves his mouth from mine and kisses my neck. I move my hand quickly, bringing him to the edge and when I know he's almost there, I guide his hard cock towards my pussy.

I am already dripping wet, the remnants of the delicious orgasm I just had and the result of our passionate kisses, and

Aidan slips inside of me with ease. He moves his hips, thrusting inside of me and I match his thrusts, needing him to go deeper, to fill me all of the way up. God I love the way he fills me up, the way we become one as he moves within me.

My orgasm is already bubbling up inside of me, threatening to spill over and leave me breathless. I can see Aidan is almost there too and so I hold myself back, waiting for him to hit his stride so we can come together. It's hard to hold myself back. I am so turned on and my body is thrumming with the need to come, but I manage it. Just barely.

As Aidan's face contorts with pleasure and he makes a low moaning sound in the back of his throat, I let go and pleasure floods my whole body. My pussy tightens around Aidan's rigid cock and he moans again as my tightness draws his orgasm out, making it more intense and making it last longer than it usually would. I grip Aidan to me with my thighs as another wave of pleasure washes over me, and then I start to come down, drifting down lazily on a bed of sated warmth.

Aidan kisses me quickly on the mouth and then he pushes himself up. I watch his chest muscles and his arm muscles as they tighten when he pushes himself up. His body is fantastic and I want to reach out and touch it, to lick him all over.

"I really do need to get in the shower now," he says.

"I know," I smile. "Go."

I watch him as he wraps my discarded towel around his waist and then he leaves the room. I lay in place on the bed for a moment and then I get up and start to get dressed. I pick Aidan's clothes up from the floor where they fell last night and lay them out on the bed for him. When he comes back to get dressed, I am blow drying my hair.

Aidan dresses quickly and then comes over to me. He stands behind me and leans down and kisses my neck. Shivers go through me as his lips run over my skin. He pulls back from me and I know he felt the shivers too, but I also know he has to leave whether we like it or not.

"I can just about make it to work on time if I leave now," he says. "See you at six?"

"See you at six," I confirm before he kisses me again and then jogs away.

I hear him say a quick hello and goodbye to Nadia as he cuts through the living room. I hope we didn't disturb her last night. Or this morning. I can't help but smile as I think of last night and this morning. God Aidan is a machine. He can make me come effortlessly and I love having sex with him. It's been no more than twenty minutes since we last had sex and already I'm counting down the minutes until six o'clock when I can see him again, have sex with him again. My pussy is getting wet again just thinking about it. I imagine Aidan's hands on me, his lips on me.

I shake my head, shaking away the images. I have to stop this or the day is going to drag even more than it normally would. I can't spend all day in this heightened state of arousal or I'm going to drive myself crazy.

I finish drying my hair and put my make up on and then I go through to the living room where Nadia is sitting nursing a cup of coffee and nibbling on a slice of toast while she watches an early morning talk show. She grins at me as I come in.

"There's coffee in the pot," she says.

"Thanks," I say.

I go into the kitchen and pour myself a cup of the coffee and then I come back to the living room and sit down. Nadia mutes the TV and turns to me.

"It's funny," Nadia says. "When Aidan works really late and he's back in early the next morning, he often crashes here because it's closer to the hospital and he gets a bit more sleep. But last night he came here and I'm guessing didn't get a whole lot of sleep."

I feel myself blushing and Nadia laughs.

"Oh come on Erika. You didn't expect me to believe you two just had a little slumber party did you?"

I shake my head and I feel myself smiling despite my embarrassment.

"We didn't disturb you did we?" I ask.

"Oh no, not at all. Once my head hits the pillow I'm out like a light. I swear the building could fall down around me and it wouldn't wake me up," Nadia says. She puts the last piece of her toast into her mouth and chews thoughtfully for a moment. "So you and Aidan are still getting along well then?"

I nod my head, trying to be casual, but again, my mouth betrays me. I just can't stop myself from smiling when I think of Aidan and just how well we're getting along.

"Wow you're really smitten aren't you?" Nadia says with a laugh.

There's no point in trying to deny it. It's written all over my face. I find myself nodding again and I feel my blush deepening slightly. It's a little weird talking to Aidan's sister about him.

"Yeah. I really am," I admit. "I was determined not to rush into anything, but I really think I'm falling for Aidan."

"Good," Nadia says. "Because from what I've seen, the feeling is mutual."

"Really?" I ask. I mean I know Aidan and I have great sex, but I've hardly dared to hope it's more than that to him. "How can you be so sure?"

"Well for starters, other than the times Aidan has crashed here from the hospital, I think he's been here about four times. And now it feels like he practically lives here."

"I'm sorry …" I start, but Nadia waves my apology away.

"It's not a complaint. Just an observation," she says. "Honestly Erika, I've never seen Aidan so content. And I've never known him to be even close to late for work."

"I guess I'm a bad influence on him," I grin.

"I agree, but in the best possible way," Nadia says. "He needs something in his life other than work. I was always worried he'd hit a certain age and end up settling for someone he wasn't that into, most likely someone from work, just to keep things simple. But now I'm not so sure that's how it will play out."

"Do you really think it can work between us?" I ask. "We're from such different worlds."

"I think it can if you're both willing to meet in the middle a little bit. Aidan will have to see that some things are more important than work, and you'll have to accept that sometimes, work will come first and Aidan might have to cancel plans at the last minute."

"I can do that," I say without hesitation. "I mean it's not like he works in an office or something. What he does is important and I understand that it's not the sort of job you can walk away from just because technically your shift has ended."

"That's good," Nadia says. "Because I don't think it's going to be long until Aidan officially asks you to be his girlfriend and it'll be better all round if you understand what comes with the job."

Is she right that Aidan is going to ask me to make this thing between us official? I hope she is. I mean I'm enjoying what we're doing and I love spending time with Aidan, and technically, we don't need a label to enjoy what we're doing together, but it would be nice to make it official. It would be nice to know that he is mine and mine alone.

"I'd like that," I smile. "And I think I know what I'm getting into. And if he does have to work late when I wasn't expecting it and he makes it up to me like he did last night, I'll be one happy little lady."

I realize I've probably said too much but Nadia just laughs.

"So have you two got any plans for tonight?" Nadia asks me.

"Yeah. I'm meeting him after work and then we're going to his place for dinner," I say.

Nadia smiles knowingly and I feel myself blushing again. It really is quite strange telling her about Aidan and me seeing as he's her brother. It's nice to be able to talk about him though, but then when I talk about him and tonight's plans, I start to think about what I know will come after the dinner, and I really don't want to think about Aidan like that in front of Nadia. That will be way too weird. I decide to change the subject before things spiral and get really awkward.

"What about you?" I ask. "Have you got any plans for tonight?"

"Actually I'm going on a date," she says with a hint of a smile.

"Oh really. Tell me more," I say, glad to be the one out if the spotlight for a moment.

"There's not really a lot to tell at this point," Nadia says. "It's our first date. I gave him my number a couple of days ago and I didn't really think he would call, but he did, and yeah. We're going to see a movie and then we're going to a bar he knows for drinks afterwards."

"Why didn't you think he would call? Look at you. You're gorgeous," I say.

It's Nadia's turn to blush slightly and she shakes her head.

"I don't know about that," she says. "Plus, I met him at the gym so when we were talking I was covered in a layer sweat and I probably looked pretty gross."

"That's a good think though," I say. "If he saw you like that and he still wants to see you again, imagine what he's going to be like when you sees you all done up tonight."

185

"I'm kind of hoping it works that way," Nadia laughs. She drains the last of her coffee and stands up. "Well I'd best get going to work. God today is going to be a long day."

I know exactly what she means about that. At least she has work to keep her distracted from watching the clock. Lord knows what I'm going to do.

After Nadia has gone, I wash out our cups and brew a fresh pot of coffee. I skip breakfast – I'm not hungry at all. I go through some of the options for what I could do today, and in the end, I settle on a Twilight movie marathon. It feels like a guilty pleasure kind of a day, and hopefully it will distract me from thinking constantly of Aidan and making the day drag by even more slowly. I know it probably won't work that way, but I have to do something and nothing is going to completely stop me thinking of Aidan.

~

It's finally time for me to leave to meet Aidan. Ok, technically, it's a little early, but if I have a nice slow walk over to the hospital, then it will be near enough time for him to finish when I get there. I'd rather be a bit early and have to wait a while than be stuck cooped up in here watching the clock any longer.

Nadia is in her room getting ready for her date and I stick my head out into the hallway.

"I'm off Nadia. Have a good night tonight," I shout.

"Thanks. You too," she replies.

I leave the apartment building and begin walking towards the hospital. It's a cool, crisp day and I pull my jacket around myself to keep the chill out. I soon start to feel warm with the walking though and I relax my arms, letting my jacket fall back into place at my sides. I wonder vaguely if I should have worn jeans now that it's getting a little chilly, but I'm glad I didn't. I'm wearing a tight black pencil skirt that sits just above my knee and I know I look good in it and I want to look good for Aidan. I can live with being a bit chilly. It's not like we're going to be standing around outside.

I check my watch as I see the hospital looming up ahead. I'm fifteen minutes early. That's not bad. I managed to kill more time than I expected on the walk over here. I debate waiting at Aidan's car, but then I decide against it. Purple legs covered in goose bumps isn't a good look for anyone. I decide to go up to Aidan's floor and wait in his office.

I head for the main doors and start towards the elevators. I am almost up to them when I hear someone calling my name. I turn around and see a woman who looks vaguely familiar to me, but I can't quite place her. She beckons to me. I am a little bit confused about what she could possibly want with me, but I go towards her, curious. As I get closer, I realize who she is. It's Stacy. She's not in scrubs. She must be just coming on shift and hasn't gotten around to changing into her scrubs yet. I am still a little confused about what she might want with me, but I guess I am about to find out. I am a little bit nervous as I approach her and she looks me up and down. I tell myself I'm being silly and I smile at her. She doesn't return my smile, but I press on with my planned opening, trying to sound normal.

"Sorry," I smile. "I didn't recognize you without your scrubs."

"You're here to see Aidan?" she says, ignoring what I said.

I'm a little bit taken aback by her bluntness and I'm not sure if what she said is a question or a statement, but I nod my head anyway. Stacy nods back.

"I thought so. Look Erika you seem like a nice enough girl and so I'm going to level with you. If you keep hanging around Aidan, you're going to end up getting hurt. Aidan and I kind of have a thing going on you see," she says. I frown. Is she seriously threatening me? She goes on. "We sleep together now and again, and we say it's a no strings thing, but we both know that's not strictly true. We're sowing our wild oats with other people, but when we're done with that, we'll come back together."

I can feel my heart breaking ever so slightly, but I don't want to give Stacy the satisfaction of seeing that she's bothering me.

"It sounds to me like you're the wild oat," I say. "You sleep together now and again and Aidan tells you its no strings attached and then you try to put some meaning to it. It's a bit sad really."

Stacy laughs and shakes her head.

"You still don't get it do you? I didn't want to have to be so crude as to spell it out to you, but I will. Doctors sometimes screw around with girls like you, girls who don't get it. But when they're ready to settle down, they marry the nurses."

She turns and walks away from me before I can answer her. I stand in place watching her walk away, blinking hard to keep the tears back. Stacy glances back at me and smiles, a fake sympathetic smile that makes me want to run over there and punch her in her smug little mouth.

"You can't have him Erika. Find your own man," she says.

I stand in place for a moment longer debating what to do and then I turn around and head back out of the hospital. I need to get away from this place so I can think clearly without getting concerned sideways glances from strangers.

I cut across the parking lot, heading back towards the apartment and then I change my mind. I stop and turn around, heading in the opposite direction now instead. I know Nadia has a date tonight, but she could still be home now and I really can't face her right now. I make my way back to my house instead. I just to be alone for a while, somewhere familiar where I can lick my wounds and try to accept what I've just been told.

I let myself into the house and I go through to the living room and sit down. I am shaking and I feel a little bit sick. I spend a few minutes sitting still, just taking deep breaths to try and get the sickly feeling to pass. When it does, I ask myself if Stacy was even telling me the truth. I want to tell myself she wasn't, but I feel like I'm just deluding myself. This whole thing with Aidan has felt too good to be true since it started and all Stacy has done is remind me of that fact.

The thing is, Aidan and I have never said we're exclusive and for that reason, he is perfectly within his rights to do what he wants with Stacy, but that doesn't make the idea of them fucking hurt any less. For all we haven't talked about being exclusive, some of the things Aidan said to me, things about him never feeling this way about anyone before, they made me think what we had was special. And surely if he thought what we had was special too then he wouldn't be fucking around with other girls while we're sort of seeing each other.

I think about Nadia telling me she's never seen Aidan this happy before and how she was convinced he was going to ask me to be his girlfriend soon. Was she in on Aidan's deception? No I tell myself. I don't think she was. There was no reason for her to say any of that stuff if she didn't really think it was true. And I'm guessing the other women Aidan has dabbled with haven't moved in with Nadia. Aidan could have always seemed this way with the new women he was sleeping with and Nadia just didn't know about it. That makes sense. More sense than thinking Nadia is somehow involved in some crazy plot to deceive me into sleeping with her brother.

I want to convince myself that Stacy is lying all the same, but the more I think about it, the more I can't see why she would have any reason to lie to me. What would she achieve by pushing me away from Aidan if the part about them sleeping together wasn't true? If Aidan genuinely isn't into her, then my not being around isn't going to magically make him want her. Surely she would know that.

Tears spring to my eyes again when I finally let myself accept that I've been played for a fool. I just wish Aidan had been honest with me. I wasn't looking for anything serious myself and I would have been happy to hook up with him and have a bit of fun. I just wouldn't have let myself get attached to him. But he implied there was more to it than that, that what we had was going somewhere, and I did let myself get attached, and now I have to accept that I'm a fool. A fool who was letting myself see Aidan in my future when he saw me as only a pit stop on his way to shacking up with Stacy.

I try to tell myself I'm not going to get angry or upset, but it's too late for that. I'm upset to know that Aidan has been sleeping with Stacy obviously, but I think more than that, I'm upset that he lied to me about it. He had a chance to come clean when we talked in his office yesterday, but he chose to tell me it was just her flirting with him, that he didn't think of her that way at all. Even if he wasn't ready to admit that there might be something between them, he didn't have to outright lie to my face like that. He could have just pointed out that we weren't exclusive and left it at that.

My phone rings, pulling my attention out of my head for a moment. I take it out of my hand bag and glance at the screen. It's Aidan. I can't talk to him right now. Maybe not ever again. I let the phone ring. A couple of seconds later, a text pings in. I want to ignore it, but I already know I won't be able to do that and so I give in and open it and read it.

"Hey. I guess you're running a little late? I'm done with work and I'll meet you at my car. X"

Have a nice wait I think to myself. Maybe you'll work out I'm not coming and go back upstairs and have a nice talk with fucking Stacy. Maybe you'll even kiss her. Ugh. What does he even see in her? Despite the fact that she's drop dead gorgeous and has a body to die for of course.

My phone rings again and I go to cut the call off, but I'm surprised to see that this time, the caller is Jeremy. I debate answering it. Maybe I should give him another chance. I mean sure, there was no spark between us, but is that really the most important thing to look for in a relationship? Aidan and I have a great spark between us, and look where that's gotten me. At least Jeremy was faithful to me. Sure we had our problems. As Jennifer pointed out, he was never really comfortable with me seeing my friends when we were together. But is that such a bad thing? Didn't it just mean he wanted to spend more time with me?

I go to hit answer, but then I remember that look of rage on Jeremy's face when I told him I liked Aidan and I pull my hand back from the screen. Aidan might have turned out to be a mistake, but that doesn't make Jeremy less of a mistake. I don't want to be with someone who makes me nervous any more than I want to be with someone who plays me for a fool.

The phone stops ringing and it makes a beeping sound telling me that I have a new voicemail. I pick it up and listen to the voicemail.

"Hi Erika, its Jeremy. I just wanted to apologize again for the other day. I shouldn't have put pressure on you like that. It's just hard knowing you've moved on. Anyway, I hope I haven't ruined everything and that we can still be friends. Give me a call when you get this, just to let me know that you're ok. That we're ok."

I shake my head as I cut off the voicemail and the phone starts to ring again. It's Aidan again this time. I'm starting to feel overwhelmed by the calls, the messages. I never thought having two men vying for my attention would be so upsetting. But one of them is someone I have decided is bad news and the other one is someone who betrayed my trust. With an angry stab of my finger, I switch my phone off.

I feel slightly better for doing it but it doesn't help me feel better about my situation as a whole. At least being here and being so riled up about Aidan has stopped me being afraid to be in the house. That's a good thing. Maybe I should try and hold onto a little bit of my anger, because I really don't see how I can go back to living with Nadia now and having to see Aidan whenever he comes over to see Nadia.

I decide I've wasted enough time crying over Aidan and I stand up and move through to the kitchen. I open the cupboard beneath the sink and pull out my cleaning supplies. If I'm going to be moving back in here, it's going to need a good cleaning, and now is as good a time as any to get started on that.

AIDAN

I can feel my nerves starting to tingle as I call Erika for the third time. I curse and cut off the call when I get a recorded message informing me that her phone is switched off. I'd like to think her battery just died, but it's too much of a coincidence that her battery died at the moment she's late to meet me and her phone was on a couple of minutes ago, even if she chose not to take my call.

I don't know why she would be avoiding my calls or messages. I mean what can have changed between us since this morning? And this morning, she was more than eager to come and meet me tonight. Hell she even convinced me to be a few minutes late for work so we could have a bit more time together this morning.

I don't want to jump to conclusions, but I can't help but worry that something is wrong. And of course my first thought is Jeremy. What if she agreed to see him again and he's convinced her to blow me off? Or worse, what if he turned up at the apartment and forced his way in and he's the one who has taken her phone away from her and turned it off?

I realize I am probably being paranoid, but I can't help it. Jeremy has shown me his true colors, and I wouldn't put anything past him at this point.

I pace up and down beside my car, torn as to what to do. I want to go over to Nadia's place to look for Erika or for some clue as to what might have happened to her. But at the same time, I am still trying to tell myself that I'm over reacting and everything is fine and Erika is just running late. If I just leave and she turns up, we might end up missing each other. And if her battery has died, we won't be able to call each other and work out a new plan to meet up.

I wait another couple of minutes and then I get into my car. I can't just stand here doing nothing. It's making me crazy. And if this is something to do with Jeremy, anything could be happening to Erika while I hang around here trying to decide what to do. I will just keep my eyes open as I drive and if it does turn out that she's just running late, I'll likely pass her on the street and I can just stop and pick her up. I won't even have to tell her I went crazy for a moment. I'll just say I figured she was running late and wanted to save her rushing.

I feel a little bit better now I've made a decision and I pull out of the parking lot and head for Nadia's building. I keep scanning the streets looking for Erika. Twice I think I see her and start to pull over, but both times, I am wrong. By the time I reach Nadia's building, I know I'm driving too fast, but I'm more concerned about Erika than the possibility of getting a speeding ticket.

I park the car, jump out and run to the building door. I don't bother ringing the bell. If Jeremy has Erika in there, he's not going to just let me in. Instead, I use my key and run into the building. I don't wait around for the elevator. It would probably be quicker to use it than to take the stairs, but standing waiting for it would feel like I was just wasting time. I run up the stairs, taking them two at a time, and by the time I reach Nadia's floor, I am a little breathless.

I still have my keys in my hand and I manage to find the right one after a moment of trying. I fumble Nadia's door open. It slams off the wall and bounces back on itself, slamming shut. I don't pause to inspect the wall to see if I've done any damage. I run down the hallway as the front door bursts open. Nadia stands in the door way. Her expression goes from seriously pissed off to concerned when she sees me and I know I must look like I've lost my mind.

"Jeez Aidan, what's going on?" she says.

"Is Erika here?" I demand.

"What? No. What happened?" she replies.

I take a deep breath and follow her into the living room when she turns and walks away from me, beckoning for me to follow her.

"Erika was meant to meet me after work. She didn't show up and her phone is switched off," I say.

"Maybe she's running late and her battery died," Nadia says.

"Or maybe something happened to her. Have you seen her at all today?"

"Well yeah. I was here when she left. She seemed fine," she says. "Aidan tell me what's really going on here. Something must have happened for you to assume the worst like this."

"I need to call the police," I say.

"No you don't. Erika is a grown woman who has been missing for less than half an hour. They're not going to take to you seriously. What you need to do is calm down and tell me what's happening," Nadia says.

Somehow, her calm voice gets through to me a little bit and I take a deep breath and sit down heavily on the couch. I tell her about Jeremy, about my suspicions about him and about how Erika said she felt afraid of him when they met up for coffee.

"I think he might have taken her," I say.

Nadia sits down beside me.

"Or she's standing in the hospital parking lot wondering where the hell you are," she says. "Or she popped home for something. Or she got her wires crossed and thought she was meant to be meeting you at your place."

"I could believe that if it wasn't for the fact that her phone is switched off," I say.

"Have you done anything to piss her off?" Nadia asks.

"No," I say. "I mean I don't think so. And you said she was fine when she left here. I haven't spoken to her or seen her to do anything to piss her off in that time. I really think I should call the police. If I explain to them about Jeremy and that she has been recently attacked, they might take it a bit more seriously."

"They might, but if it's nothing, and I suspect that's the case, then this is only going to cause trouble. And I don't mean for Jeremy. If half of what you've said about him is right then screw him – he deserves everything he gets. I mean because it'll cause trouble for you. How is Erika going to feel if the police pick her up because she got confused about where she was meant to be meeting you? She'll think you've lost your mind."

"I know you're right," I say after a second. "But what am I supposed to do? I can't just sit here and hope she shows up eventually."

"You go back to the hospital and then to your place. I'll go to her house. And if she isn't in any of those places, then we'll take it from there," Nadia says.

I open my mouth to agree with her, but then I take in the fact that she's wearing a dress and heels and I realize she was likely on her way out.

"You don't have to do that. I can swing by Erika's place too," I say. "You're on your way out somewhere."

"It's just a date. I can reschedule it," she says.

I shake my head.

"No honestly, you go out and have a good time. I'm sure you're right about this. I'm sure I am just being paranoid and I don't want to ruin your night."

"But ..." Nadia starts.

"How about this?" I interrupt her. "If I don't find Erika in the next hour, I'll call you and then you can come and help me deal with this."

"Ok," Nadia agrees. "Let me know if you do find her as well though."

"I will," I reassure her.

I get up to leave, already wondering which place to go to first to search. I decide to start back at the hospital in case she really was just late and is there. I can't see her being there now though. If she saw my car had gone, would she have just stood in the parking lot?

I hurry back to the hospital and have a quick drive through the grounds and around both the staff parking lot and the normal parking lot. There's no sign of Erika. I think the next most likely place to look for her if everything is ok and normal will be my place. Like Nadia said, she might have gotten her wires crossed and thought she was meant to be meeting me there. But even though that makes the most logical sense, her place is closer and I decide to go there first.

I pull up outside of her house and I see instantly that there's a light on in one of the windows. The sight of that light makes me feel both better and worse. Better because at least now I'm confident I've found her, and worse because her being here isn't a misunderstanding. She clearly doesn't want to see me for some reason. And I'm beginning to think that Jeremy might not be the reason for it. I don't know what is, but why would Jeremy bring her here of all places if he had taken her?

I spot movement behind the curtains, someone passing the window, and I know by the silhouette its Erika. I pick up my phone and send Nadia a quick text saying I've found Erika. She texts back quickly saying she's relieved and wishing me a good night. I'm not sure that's likely to happen, but I send back a similar sentiment. I really don't want to ruin Nadia's night now that I know Erika is safe.

I sit in the car for a moment longer. Now I am confident Erika is safe, I'm putting off approaching her, because I have a feeling that whatever is going on is something that's going to break my heart. Maybe she thinks we're moving too fast and she wants to cool things off a bit. That would hurt, but it wouldn't be as bad as her wanting to end things with me altogether.

I tell myself I could be blowing this all out of proportion and I won't know for sure what's going on until I get brave enough to get out of the car and go and talk to her. My stomach is whirling as I get out of the car and walk up Erika's short garden path.

I knock on the door and I wait. I don't have long to wait before the door is pulled open.

"Erika ..." I start.

She doesn't respond. She barely even looks at me. She starts to close the door in my face. The last thing I want to do is force my way inside and scare her, but I can't just let her shut me out like this. I need to know what's going on here, what has changed between us since this morning.

"Erika, wait," I say. I reach up and put my hand on the door, stopping it from closing but not trying to force it open wider. "Please talk to me. Tell me what's going on."

"I have nothing to say to you Aidan. Remove your hand from my door please," Erika says.

Her voice is cold, not like her usual voice, and it hurts me so much to hear her using that tone on me. I'm not ready to give up on her though. I don't think I'll ever be ready to give up on her. I guess Jeremy and I are similar in that sense, although I would never resort to hurting Erika.

"We need to talk about whatever has happened Erika," I say.

She sighs and stops pushing on the door. She doesn't exactly invite me inside, but she walks away, leaving the door open behind her. I step inside and close the door and follow her through another door into her living room. I am conscious that this is the first time I've been to her place. I never thought that the first time I saw her house would be like this.

"Tell me what's wrong," I say.

Erika sits down on the couch and shakes her head. I sit beside her and she shuffles away from me slightly, leaving a gap between us. A gap I don't like one little bit.

"I'm not mad at you. Not really," she says. "I'm mad at myself for being stupid enough to actually think you might be different."

I have to admit that one throws me. I have no idea what she's talking about.

"Erika I don't know what's happened or why you're suddenly so mad at me. Or not mad at me, whatever. Please just tell me what I'm supposed to have done," I say.

"You really didn't think I'd find out did you? I mean I know I really can't complain about it. We never said we were exclusive, but I don't want to be with someone who is just playing the field Aidan. I'm sorry."

She thinks I'm sleeping with someone else? Now I'm really lost. Where the hell has this come from all of a sudden?

"I don't know what you're talking about Erika. You sound like you think I'm sleeping with someone else," I say.

"I don't just think you're sleeping with someone else. I know you are. She told me Aidan. You can drop the act," Erika says.

Tears come to her eyes as she says it and I want so badly to wrap her up in my arms and tell her everything will be ok, that I haven't so much as looked at another woman since I met her. Something tells me that would be a bad move though. I think if I try to touch her now, she'll just get mad and push me away and she might refuse to talk about this with me at all, and I need her to talk to me about it. I need to find out what's gotten into her so I can fix it.

"I don't know who has told you what, but I promise you that I'm not sleeping with anyone else," I say.

"Right. So you and Stacy don't have some arrangement where you both play the field a bit and sleep together and then one day end up together?" Erika says.

"What? No, we don't fuck," I say. I snap a little bit which I don't mean to, but I'm getting a little bit annoyed that Erika has jumped to this conclusion because she saw Stacy flirting with me once. "Where on earth have you gotten that idea from?"

"I came to the hospital to meet you after work. I was a little early so I was coming up to your office. I ran into Stacy and she told me that's what is happening here," Erika says.

"And you believed her?" I say.

She blushes a little and then she gives a little sniff and nods her head.

"Well yeah. I mean she's smoking hot. Why wouldn't you be into her?" she says. "And why would she make something like that up?"

"Look Erika, Stacy has a bit of a crush on me. She flirts and drops hints that she'd like us to be more than just colleagues. I had no idea she would go this far though. But I promise you nothing has ever happened between Stacy and me and nothing ever will."

"Really?" Erika says.

She's finally looking me in the eye and I can see that she wants to believe me, but I don't think she's quite there yet.

"Really," I say. "Why would I want Stacy when I'm in love with you?"

Fuck. I didn't mean to say that. Erika looks at me, her mouth hanging open in surprise.

"Shit, I'm sorry," I say. "It's far too early to say that, and …"

"I love you too," Erika interrupts me. She gives a soft laugh. "It is far too early to say it, but it doesn't change the way I feel."

I move closer to her and this time, she makes no effort to move away from me. Instead, she comes towards me. Our arms reach out and wrap around each other, our lips meeting. Erika tastes of her salty tears and her usual sweet taste, a taste I have come to know and love.

I kiss her like I have never kissed her before. I want my kiss to tell her all of the things that my words can't say strongly enough. I want my kiss to tell her without doubt that she's the only girl for me.

She kisses me back as ferociously as I kiss her. Our lips are pressed together so hard it's almost painful, and I still don't feel like I'm close enough to her. I want to devour her, to have every inch of her merge with every inch of me. I want to be one with her. Now and forever.

Her hands move down my back and come around to my front. She reaches for my belt, opening it and then moving on to my jeans. Within seconds, she has my cock free. I lift my ass from the couch long enough for her to pull my jeans and my boxer shorts down my thighs.

She straddles me, pushing her skirt up around her waist. She pulls back from the kiss we still share and looks me in the eye for a moment. Her chest is rising and falling quickly, her breath coming in short pants. She leans in and kisses me again.

I run my hands up her thighs and then I grab the side of her panties and pull hard on them, tearing the fabric. Erika pulls back from my lips long enough to gasp and then she giggles and kisses me again.

I don't waste any time. I can't wait another moment to make love to Erika, to let her know she's the only woman I want to make love to ever again. I push her torn panties aside and run my fingers over her clit. She's dripping wet and as ready for this as I am. I begin to work her clit with my fingers, but she reaches down, grabs my wrist and pushes my hand away.

I'm worried for a moment, afraid she's changed her mind, but instead of climbing off me, she reaches down for my cock and positions herself above it. She lowers herself, impaling herself on my cock and I know now why she moved my hand aside. She just wanted to feel me inside of her. She was as desperate for us to connect as I was.

She begins to move herself up and down on my cock, her smooth, slippery walls caressing me. I feel pleasure begin to spread through my body, radiating out of my every pore. I have to bite down on the inside of my mouth to stop myself from climaxing too soon.

I move my hips in time with Erika's movements, letting her set the pace. She's not teasing me, not trying to make this last. She throws herself into the rhythm, her desperation as apparent as mine as she works herself into a frenzy on top me.

Suddenly, she stops moving. She sits still on my lap, my cock in her pussy's grip as it tightens around me. Erika throws her head back and makes an animalistic sound as her orgasm tears through her body. I push my fingers between her lips and press down on her clit, making her orgasm last longer, feel more intense.

She's rigid, her head still back, barely even breathing. Her hands have turned to fists and she tugs on my hair as she comes hard. I feel her pussy tightening around me again and then a flood of her juices soak my lap. I moan low in the back of my throat as her heat douses me.

She lifts her head back up and looks at me for a moment and then she begins to move again. She is so wet, so tight. I can feel my cock tingling as my own climax comes rushing on. I try to slow myself down, to hold back a little so that this can last longer, but I can't do it. Erika is consuming me so completely that I lose control of myself.

I am so close to the edge that I just can't stop myself from wanting to go over. I move my hips faster, filling Erika fully, stretching her pussy out and making her take my full length time after time. She is gasping and writhing and when I hit my climax, she spasms around me again as she has another orgasm herself.

We are both moaning, our hands all over each other as pleasure floods us. I feel like I'm floating away from my body, from the anchor to the world. I am filled with a euphoria so deep it's almost spiritual. And then I'm coasting down, my body warm and relaxed.

Erika collapses against my chest and I wrap my arms around her as she pants. Her body is shaking slightly as she tries to get herself back under control. I slip out of her, already missing the warm glove of her pussy, but I enjoy the feeling of just holding her in my arms, and I clutch her tightly to me as I slowly coast down from the ecstasy that filled me only moments ago and come back to myself.

After a few minutes, Erika lifts her head from my shoulder and smiles at me. She kisses my lips, a soft kiss, and then she climbs off my lap. She stands up for a moment and takes off her shredded panties, pushing them into her hand bag, and then she pulls her skirt down and sits back down. I follow her lead, pulling my boxer shorts and jeans back up and fastening my button, zipper and belt. I sit back down beside her and we look at each for a moment before Erika finally shakes her head slightly.

"I can't believe I almost threw away what we have because of some jealous little bitch who was just trying to make trouble for us. I never should have believed a word she said. At least not without asking you for the truth," she says. "Are you mad at me because I ignored your calls instead of talking to you about it?"

"No," I say, although that's not strictly true. I decide I don't want to lie to Erika ever and I change my answer. "A little bit maybe. But I get it. We haven't known each other for that long and I can't expect you to just trust me instantly."

"I'm sorry," she says.

I reach out and take her hand.

"It's ok," I say. "There's no harm done. And maybe this will give us a chance to really talk and establish some ground rules. How about we make a promise to each other right now that we'll never lie to each other?"

"I like that," Erika smiles. "And I think we should also say that if something happens that upsets one of us, or makes us feel insecure, that we should agree to talk to each other about it. You know, instead of going into hiding like I did."

"Yes, I like that idea," I smile. "Because I was really worried about you when you wouldn't take my calls. So how about this? If you're too mad to talk to me in that moment, just send me a text message saying that so that I know you're ok."

Erika smiles and shakes her head.

"You don't need to worry about me so much Aidan. I know there was the attack, but even the police think there's very little chance of that happening again. I don't want to worry you any time I miss a call."

I know I should tell her about Jeremy, about why I was so worried, but the last thing I want right now is another argument. And it's not like I'm lying to her. She hasn't mentioned Jeremy. If she outright asks if this has something to do with him, then I'll be honest with her, but I know she won't, because she doesn't consider Jeremy to be dangerous. She just thinks of him as a nuisance.

"I'll try to dial it back a bit," I smile.

She leans in and kisses me again.

"Good, because I have no intention of going anywhere and I need you to believe that," she says.

"I do," I promise her. And again, that's not a lie. I do trust her not to run out on me again.

I stand up and Erika looks up at me, a look of confusion on her face.

"Come on," I say. "It's not too late to salvage the night and have dinner. Assuming you're hungry of course."

"I'm starving," Erika grins.

"Let's go out to eat," I say. "I'll take you somewhere nice and we'll have a nice meal, and then we'll go back to my place after it."

"That sounds good," Erika says.

"Don't you want to put some panties on?" I ask as she stands up and walks towards the door.

"No. I don't think I do," she says with a flirty smile. "I kind of like the idea of you knowing I'm naked beneath my skirt."

I moan as desire floods me.

"Be careful Erika," I grin. "We might not even get to the restaurant if you keep talking like that."

She laughs and ducks away from me as I grab for her. The second time, she lets me catch her and I kiss her long and deep and then pull away, leaving her breathless.

"Now we both have something to think about over dinner," I grin.

"Oh that's cruel," Erika laughs.

I wake up to Erika shaking me.

"It's almost seven o'clock," she says. "We've overslept. You're going to be late for work."

I roll over and smile at her.

"I'm off today," I tell her. "I thought maybe we could do something later on if you fancied it?"

"Oh dammit, I can't today," Erika replies. "I assumed you would be working so I made plans with Jennifer for this afternoon."

"And tonight?" I ask.

"Tonight I'm all yours," Erika grins at me.

I pull her into my arms.

"Good," I say.

I kiss her and then push the sheet back.

"I don't have to meet Jennifer until lunch time. We could still do something now," Erika says, making it clear with her raised eyebrow what she's referring to when she says we could do something now.

I grin at her and pull the sheet back over myself.

"I do have something I need to do this morning, but it can wait a little while longer," I tell her.

"What do you have to do?" she asks.

I sigh. I didn't really want to tell her what I'm planning on doing but we promised each other we wouldn't lie to each other and so I decide to be honest. She probably won't like the idea, but it has to be done.

"I'm going to the hospital to have a word with Stacy about her staying the hell out of my business," I say.

"Oh God no, please don't do that," Erika says. "I don't want her to know she got to me."

I kiss the tip of her nose and smile.

"Don't worry. I'm not going to give her the satisfaction of thinking she got under your skin. I'm going to tell her we laughed at how pathetic she is. But I do need to have a conversation with her though. What she did crossed a major line and I want to make it clear to her that she is to stay out of my life from now on," I say.

"I guess it will be kind of fun to have her think her little plan did nothing but amuse us," Erika admits.

"Exactly," I grin. "Now do you want to talk about Stacy, or you want me to kiss you?"

"Oh that's a tough one," Erika grins.

She purses her mouth up like she's thinking. I can't wait any longer for her to make her decision so I take it out of her hands by leaning closer and fitting my mouth over hers. She wraps her arms around me and pulls me closer, confirming the decision was the right one.

AIDAN

I check my watch as I pull up in the hospital parking lot. Its good timing. That extra half an hour I spent with Erika this morning was good for two reasons. The first and most important reason was obviously because I got to spend more time with Erika and I got to make her come so hard her eyes rolled back in her head. The second and slightly less important reason is because I have managed to time it so that Stacy is about due to come off shift. If I had had to, I would have taken her into my office and had this conversation with her while she was working, but its better that I can have it when she's off the clock really. It feels a little bit unprofessional to have the conversation in work time, despite the fact that Stacy seemingly caused the problem while she was on her way into work.

I pull my phone out of my pocket and send Stacy a text message asking her to meet me in the staff canteen when she's finished work for the day. I don't say why. If I do, I'm pretty sure she wouldn't come to meet me. She's probably thinking that I'm going to confess my undying love for her or something. Oh well, she's going to be disappointed then isn't she.

I don't wait for Stacy to reply. I just throw my phone on the passenger seat and get out of the car and head for the canteen. I know she won't be able to resist coming to see what I want.

I slip into the canteen and order a coffee and go to sit down at a table that's far enough away from the others to be marginally private, but that is easily visible from the counter so that Stacy will see me. I can feel my temper starting to rise as I sip my coffee and look out of the window. Stacy's meddling could have caused Erika and me to break up and I want nothing more than to blast Stacy for what she did. I remind myself that's not the way to play this. I don't want her to be able to take any satisfaction from her little stunt, and besides that, I don't want her to know that Erika and I are still so fragile that her little game almost worked on us and ruined what we have.

I look up as a shadow falls across the table. Stacy grins at me and sits down opposite me. She doesn't have a drink or anything.

"What's going on?" she asks.

"I just wanted to talk to you about something," I say.

"Go on," she prompts me.

She doesn't seem in the least bit uncomfortable. She has no idea I know what she's done. She's so brazen, messing with my life, trying to get Erika to leave me, and then sitting here all sweet and innocent like nothing has happened.

"I was just curious to find out what you hoped to accomplish by lying to Erika about us sleeping together," I say.

She smiles. She actually fucking smiles.

"Oh come on Aidan. It's only a matter of time before we do. I just thought I would speed up the process. I mean neither of us is getting any younger right? And I hate to see you wasting your time on these random girls when we could be together sooner," she says.

Holy shit she really is totally fucking delusional. In her mind, what she told Erika is actually how she sees this playing out. That we both play the field for a while and then one day, we get sick of doing that and we end up together. God how have I gotten myself into this mess? I surely have never given off any sort of signal that implies that could happen.

"I have tried to save your feelings in the past Stacy, but let me make this crystal clear to you. I do not have feelings for you. I am not attracted to you. And whatever little fantasy you've built up in your head about us is never going to happen. Do you understand me?" I say.

I keep my voice low and firm, but not nasty. I don't want to hurt her. I just want her to understand that this thing she believes is between us is never going to happen. She looks down at the table and nods her head.

"And for the record, Erika isn't just some random girl," I add.

"I bet she was really mad though huh? When she thought she had some competition," Stacy says with a sly grin.

She's beyond belief. I was worrying a second ago about her feelings and now she's pulled this one out. She's quite a piece of work. Screw her feelings.

"Actually, we both thought it was pretty funny. I mean in some ways I suppose it's not funny. It's actually a little sad. Like how desperate you have to be to pull a stunt like that," I say.

"I ... I thought you liked me Aidan. I thought you just needed to be sure I felt the same way," Stacy says.

If I believed that for a second, I might be able to bring myself to feel sorry for her again, but I don't believe it. Nothing I have ever said or done could have given Stacy the impression I liked her as anything more than a colleague. When she started getting flirty with me, I made damned sure I never did anything that could be seen as me leading her on or encouraging her behavior.

"Well now you know differently," I say. "And let me make something else clear to you. We might have laughed at your little game, but don't think I'm underestimating how serious this is. You could have caused some real trouble there and I won't have you messing with my life anymore. If you ever pull another stunt like this again, or if you insist on continuing to flirt with me, I will have you fired. Do you understand me?"

"I ... Yes," Stacy says.

She looks down at the table and then back up at me. Her face is flushed now and she looks ashamed of herself. Tears sparkle in the corners of her eyes.

"I'm sorry. I don't know what I was thinking," she says. "Please don't get me fired Aidan. I really need this job."

"As long as you never try anything like this again, I won't get you fired," I say. "But don't mistake my kindness for weakness Stacy. If I get so much as a hint of you trying anything like this again, you're gone."

"I swear I won't," she says. "I really am sorry."

She gets up and practically runs from the canteen. I go back to sipping my coffee. I think I got through to her. I'll be keeping an ear out for any gossip being spread about me though, and I'm going to be very careful to not end up alone anywhere with Stacy if I can avoid it. She really is a strange girl, but she's a good nurse which is the only reason I am giving her this second chance.

I finish the last of my coffee and head out of the canteen. I really wanted to spend the day with Erika, but I wasn't going to try and get her to ditch her friend and spend time with me instead. That would have felt all too Jeremy of me. I debate what to do with myself until I see her tonight.

I walk out of the hospital still thinking about it. I have been meaning to catch up with Tim, a good friend who I don't see often enough these days, and I decide I'll call him and see if he's free for a couple of drinks this afternoon. I reach down to my pocket for my phone and I realize it's not there. I left it on the passenger seat of my car after texting Stacy. I sigh. It's no big deal though. I can call him from the car.

As I approach the car, I see that once more, Jeremy is standing by my car. At least he's not sitting on my hood today, but his keeping on turning up like this is getting damned annoying.

"What do you want?" I demand.

"Oh I was just making sure no one broke your car window to get to your phone. It's not a good idea to leave your valuables on display you know," Jeremy says.

"Cut the bullshit Jeremy. What are you doing here? Have you been following me?" I say.

He must have been or how would he have known where to find me? He ignores my question and smiles at me.

"Look Aidan, I think we misunderstood each other last time we talked," he says. "You see, I thought we had agreed that you would stay the hell away from my girl, but it seems that you missed that part."

I snort out a laugh.

"Are you kidding me? Do you really think you can intimidate me into leaving Erika?" I say.

"Well here's the thing. I was really hoping I could reason with you. And that's why I'm giving you one more chance to do the honorable thing and step aside. That's twice I've asked you nicely now and I don't intend to ask you a third time. If you continue to ignore my friendly warnings, then I'm going to have to take matters into my own hands," Jeremy says. He smiles coldly at me. "Just so we're clear and there can be no misunderstanding this time, if you don't stay away from Erika, I'm going to kill you. And then I'm going to teach her a lesson for being a filthy little whore who invited you to jump into bed with her. Is that clear enough for you?"

I can feel my temper rising to the point where I know I'm going to see red. I want to punch Jeremy right in his ugly fucking face. I want to break every last bone in his body. I want to make him feel the pain he made Erika feel, because after this last little threat, there's no doubt left in my mind that he was the one who hurt her.

"You screwed up little fucker," I start.

I take a step towards Jeremy, my fists balled up at my sides. I tell myself to calm down, to think rationally about this. As much as I'd love to knock the fuck out of Jeremy, this area is on camera and he's not worth losing my career over. And after what he did to Erika, a beating isn't enough for him. I want him to really pay. I want him to do time for what he did to her.

A plan starts to form in my mind. A way I can make that happen and I back off slightly. I smile at Jeremy and he frowns.

"You think this is funny?" he demands.

"Not particularly," I shrug. "In fact, I think it's pretty sad that Erika has made it so clear she doesn't want anything to do with you and you're still this hung up on her."

"She's the love of my life," Jeremy snaps. "And you're getting in the way of that. Don't you see it?"

"All I see is a sad little man who can't accept something is over," I say. "Now you've said your piece so let me say mine. Erika is with me now and nothing you can say or do can change that. I'm going out of town this evening and I won't be back until tomorrow morning. And when I come back, I'm going to ask Erika if she has seen any sign of you, and she's going to say no, because you're going to stay the hell away from her. Am I making myself clear?"

"Oh crystal clear," Jeremy says with a smug smile.

He turns and walks away without another word and I smile to myself as I get into my car. He's taken the bait. He thinks Erika will be alone in the apartment tonight and I'd bet my last dollar he's going to show up there. Now I just have to finish setting everything up to make sure he shows his true colors without Erika getting hurt.

I'm going to prove that he is dangerous and make damned sure he can never hurt Erika again.

I fire up the engine and head towards Nadia's place to tell her about my plan and get her on board with it. I guess my catch up with Tim will have to wait a little bit longer.

JEREMY

W hen Aidan told me he was going out of town for the
night, I could barely contain my excitement. I
covered myself in front of him though, telling him I understood what he was saying. I did understand what he was
saying. He was giving me a way in with Erika – a way to get
her back. That's not what he meant though when he told me
he was going out of town – he meant I should stay away
from her - and when I told him I did understand, I didn't
mean for a second I would be staying away from Erika. I
meant I understood that she would be alone, and that she
would soon be mine again. He seriously thinks I'm scared of
him and that I'll stay away from Erika. Well he's wrong. I
won't. I couldn't do it even if I wanted to. She's mine. End of
story.

I'd be willing to bet he's going to go over to the apartment to
say goodbye to Erika before he leaves, so I'm going to give it
a few hours before I go over there. My plan is to hang around
outside of the building for a while and make sure Nadia goes
out somewhere. It's a fair bet – she goes out most nights as

I've learned watching the building for signs of Erika. If Nadia doesn't end up going out tonight for whatever reason, then I'll just have to take my chances on showing up with her there. Surely if that happens, she'll see that Erika and I need some alone time and make herself scarce.

Once I have Erika alone, I know exactly what I'm going to do. I'm going to tell her about how Aidan threatened me, telling me to stay away from her and how he thinks of her as his property. Obviously I'm not going to tell her I went to the hospital to see him – I'm going to tell her he turned up at my place, that I think he's been following me. I can tell her how I've seen his car around my area a few times, and really lay it on thick, saying how I didn't want to be the one to have to tell her that her new boyfriend is a bit of psycho, but once he threatened me, I knew I had no choice but to warn her.

That will make her question everything. I know how hard it is to get Erika to act like a good girlfriend and accept that she doesn't need to see other people. I was clever when I did it though; I would tell her I had planned something special and act hurt that she wanted to be with someone else instead rather than just saying she couldn't go out with her friends. It always worked. She would feel guilty when she realized she was being a bad girlfriend and she would stay in with me. If I can convince her that Aidan isn't that sophisticated, that he threatens her friends instead, I think I can turn her against him easily enough.

Once I do that, then I think the rest will be pretty easy. See Aidan is all shiny and new, but once Erika sees that he's not the person she thinks he is, then there won't be any reason she won't want to come back to me.

This time, I'm not giving her a choice in the matter. I tried that once and it didn't work. Erika and I are meant to be together and I really thought she would see it once we'd been apart for a little while, but apparently she hasn't. Or she hadn't when I met her for coffee anyway. Maybe she has seen it by now, so I'll give her one more chance to just admit to herself and to me that we're meant to be together. I'm confident she'll take it after I tell her about Aidan.

If she doesn't, then I'm done messing around like this. I'm the best thing that ever happened to Erika and if she's too dumb to see that, then maybe she doesn't even deserve to have me. That doesn't mean she just gets to run off into the sunset with some other guy though. No chance of that. I've told her once and I'll tell her again. If I can't have her, then no one else will. And this time, I'll make damned sure I finish the job.

Fucking bitch. Rejecting me. How dare she? Who the fuck does she think she is? I'll show her what happens to stuck up bitches who suddenly think they're too good for me.

Calm down Jeremy, I tell myself. You're getting way ahead of yourself here. Erika isn't some stuck up bitch who thinks she's too good for you. She loves you. She's just too stubborn to admit that ending things with you was a mistake. You can show her that none of that matters now. You can leave the past in the past where it belongs and just look to the future, a future that belongs to you and Erika.

That thought calms me down and gives me another idea. An idea I know will get Erika back on my side and let me win her back. I smile as I turn the key in my car's ignition and pull away. I drive to the nearest shopping center and park the car. I get out and I walk to the entrance. I can feel the spring in my step, the smile on my face. I don't know why I didn't think of this sooner. I scrap the plan of painting Aidan as the bad guy. I don't need to do that. Not now. I have a much better plan now.

I am almost delirious with happiness by the time I reach the first jewelery store in the shopping center. I go inside and peer through the glass display case until I spot the perfect engagement ring. It's not cheap – it's almost three thousand dollars, but Erika is worth every penny of it.

I nod to the sales associate and let her know I'm ready to be served. She comes towards me with a wide smile.

"Can I help you?" she asks.

"Yes," I say. "I'd like to see that ring there please."

I point to the one I want. Its white gold with a large diamond set into a cluster of smaller diamonds.

"Great choice," the sales associate smiles as she slides back the glass on her side and lifts the ring from the display.

She hands it to me and I peer at it, sure it's the right one and sure that this is going to work.

"How long have you been together?" she asks me.

"Not that long," I smile. "A couple of months. But when you know you've met the one, it doesn't matter how long it's been does it?"

"Not at all," she smiles. "I think she's a very lucky girl."

Me too I think to myself. And how can she not see it when I turn up with this ring and show her that I'm in this for the long haul? That she is meant to be mine forever.

"I'll take it," I smile.

"What size do you need?" the sales associate asks as I hand her back the ring. "I can order it now and it should be here within the next two weeks."

Dammit. I hadn't considered that part. I shake my head.

"I don't know," I admit. "I want the proposal to be a surprise and there's no way to ask someone's ring size without giving the game away. Can I just take that one and if it's the wrong size, get it sized later?"

"Sure," the sales associate smiles. "In fact, hold on a moment. I have a couple more of these in the back. You can choose the one you think is the closest size to her finger. Maybe you'll get lucky and get the right size."

I thank her and she moves through a door behind the counter. I ask myself if I'm doing the right thing, and for a moment, doubt creeps in. I shake away my doubts. I need to show Erika that we're meant for each other and I know this will work. How could it not work? It'll show Erika just how serious I am about her.

The sales associate comes back with a small tray filled with several of the same rings as the one I chose. I study them for a moment and choose the one I think is the closest in size to Erika's finger. I pay for the ring and leave the store, feeling like I'm walking on air. By this time tomorrow, Erika will be mine again. We'll be engaged and starting to plan our wedding.

Now I just have to make sure I don't blow it. I get into my car and head home. In a couple of hours, I'll head to Erika's place and start watching for any signs of Nadia leaving the building. It's going to be a long wait, but getting Erika back will make it all worth it.

AIDAN

I'm almost at Nadia's place when I realize that Erika will likely be there and having her around will complicate things slightly. I don't want to tell Erika the plan as I am worried it will scare her. Or that she'll think I'm exaggerating and refuse to go along with it. No, I need to talk to Nadia alone, and it will seem strange to Erika if I turn up at the apartment and take Nadia off to talk to her in private. I pull up at the side of the road and pull my phone out and call Nadia.

"Hello?" she says.

"Hi, it's me," I reply. "Listen, don't tell Erika it's me ok?"

"Ok," she says, drawing the word out into a question.

"I need to talk to you about something important. Alone. And I need you to not mention it to Erika. Can you slip out now and come to my place with me?" I say.

"What's wrong?" she asks instantly.

"I don't want to go into it over the phone," I say. "Can you get away or not?"

"Of course," she says. "I'll leave now and meet you at your place in fifteen minutes."

I thank her and end the call and then I start the car again. I do a U-turn and head towards home. I don't like the idea of Erika being alone right now, but I don't think Jeremy will try anything this early. I told him I was leaving this evening and that buys me a few hours where he will likely assume I'll be at Nadia's place. Even if he sees my car isn't around, I don't think he'll risk going there until he's confident I am not around.

I arrive home and go inside. I don't have long to wait before Nadia arrives. I open the door and let her in. I close the door behind her and gesture for her to sit down.

"Tell me what's going on," she says. "Are you ill or something?"

"No, nothing like that," I say. "Has Erika mentioned a man named Jeremy to you?"

"Her ex boyfriend? Sure. God Aidan is this whole thing because you're jealous? Trust me, Erika is well and truly over him," Nadia replies.

"It's not that. Listen this is going to sound crazy at first, but just let me explain and don't interrupt and it will all make sense," I say.

Nadia nods for me to go on.

"I think Jeremy is the one who attacked Erika," I start.

"What? How the hell have you come to that conclusion?" Nadia interrupts me.

"I see the no interrupting thing is working well," I say.

Nadia sighs and rolls her eyes.

"Fine. Go on," she says.

"Don't you think it's a little weird that he just so happened to drop in on her within the few hours she was at her place? I think he was following her. When I met the two of them outside of your building that day, Jeremy didn't look happy at all to see me there. And when I came back out later on, there was a car across the road from your building and I think Jeremy was watching the place. When he saw me, he sped off like a maniac. Someone innocent just doesn't do that. He had scratches on his hands, and of course I realize that could be a coincidence, but they were consistent with the marks I would expect to see on someone who had been choking a person and that person was trying to get them off," I say.

I pause for a moment. Nadia doesn't look quite as skeptical as she did when I first said that I thought Jeremy was the one who attacked Erika, but she doesn't look entirely convinced about what I'm saying to her yet either.

"Twice now he has been waiting for me in the hospital parking lot when I've finished work, and both times, he's threatened me and told me to stay away from Erika. When she met him for coffee, he got angry when she refused to get back with him and she said that for a moment, she was afraid of him."

"Ok," Nadia says slowly when I finish. "He sounds like a piece of work, but if he wants Erika back so badly, why would he have hurt her?"

"My theory is that he tried to get back with her then and when she turned him down, he got angry. I swear Nadia, something is off about that guy."

She's looking at me like I've lost my mind, but then she nods her head.

"Ok. So what are we going to do about it?" she asks me.

"Wait," I say. "You believe me?"

"At first, I thought it sounded crazy, but someone attacked Erika, and I'm not buying the theory it was a stranger, not when there was no sign of forced entry. And you're not exactly known for being paranoid, so I'm going to run with you on this one. It's definitely not the sign of someone normal and balanced when he's threatened you at work. To have done that, he had to have been following you or he wouldn't have known where you worked in the first place," Nadia says.

I take a moment to digest what she's saying. It makes me feel much better to know that Nadia at least thinks this is plausible. It confirms what I really already know – I'm not just jealous. I'm onto something real here. I decide to tell Nadia exactly what Jeremy said the last time we ran into each other before I tell her what I've done and what I plan on doing next.

"The last time Jeremy collared me was a couple of hours ago. He said if I don't leave Erika alone, he will kill me and then he'll teach her a lesson for being a dirty little slut. That's what really convinced me he might have hurt her," I say.

"Holy shit," Nadia says. "We have to do something about this. I know you told me not to tell Erika I was meeting you and I haven't, but we need to tell her about this Aidan. She needs to be warned about Jeremy in case he calls her and she goes off to meet him or something."

"That was my first thought, but the more I think about it, the more I think Erika will just think I'm being jealous. I don't think she'll take the risk seriously," I say.

"So what's the plan then? Please tell me you have a better plan than keeping Erika in the dark about this and hoping it all just goes away," Nadia says.

"I do," I say. "When Jeremy was making his little threats, I really wanted to put the fucker on his ass, but I told myself it needed to be more permanent than that ..."

"Jeez Aidan," Nadia interrupts me.

I roll my eyes at her.

"I'm not planning on murdering him. Although I admit I made it sound that way. No I plan on getting him prosecuted for what he did to Erika and I plan on him going to prison for it," I tell her.

"How are you going to do that? You have no evidence he's anything but a bit of a creep and he's hardly likely to confess is he?" Nadia says.

"I've set something up for tonight," I say. "I told Jeremy I was going out of town tonight and warned him to stay away from Erika. If I'm right about this, he won't be able to resist going to your place tonight. I need you to go out. I figure he'll be watching the place from around six, so you go out shortly after six so he thinks Erika is alone."

"What will that prove? He's made no secret of the fact he wants her back," Nadia says. "You can hardly call the police and tell them your girl's ex turned up to win her back and you want him arrested."

"I won't be there when he arrives," I say. "I'm confident that Erika will tell him to get lost, and I think he'll make a move to attack her again."

"No Aidan," Nadia says, shaking her head firmly. "This could get too far out of hand. What if she gets hurt again?"

"I'm planning on having the police waiting in your room. At the first sign of trouble, they'll come out and arrest Jeremy," I say. "I need you to take Erika somewhere when I call you and confirm the time so the police can get into place."

"This is all a bit much Aidan. What if the police don't agree to do this? Then Erika is in real danger," Nadia says.

"Do you really think I haven't thought of that? If the police refuse to come, I'll take Erika to my place and then I'll tell her everything," I say.

"Ok. I don't think the police will agree to this, but ..."

"I do," I interrupt her. "They know I'm a doctor, and while I don't like to play the doctor card, it does bring a certain level of professional respect with it. I think they'll take me seriously on this one. And it's not like they have anything else to go on is it? If they refuse to spend an hour or so waiting to see if they can catch Erika's attacker, it won't do much for their image as people who actually want to solve crimes."

Nadia sighs and nods her head.

"Ok, maybe it will work."

"What was your but earlier? You said you don't think the police will agree to this, but," I say.

"But what if they do agree to it and then Jeremy doesn't even show up?" she asks.

"Then I'll have to eat a lot of humble pie," I say. "And I will assume I was wrong about Jeremy and let this whole thing go."

"Ok," Nadia agrees. "If the police agree, let me know and I'll take Erika out somewhere. And don't forget to tell her that you're going to be out of town tonight or she'll wonder where you are."

I thank Nadia and she leaves my place. Now comes the hard part. Convincing Officer Prescott of my theory.

～

Everything is in place. I called the police station and established that Officer Prescott was there. I decided I had a better chance of convincing her this was for real face to face and so I drove down to the station and spoke to her. She was a little bit skeptical at first, but I managed to convince her that it was at least possible that Jeremy was Erika's attacker after I told her the full story. Eventually, she agreed to go along with my plan.

I let Nadia know when Officer Prescott and I would be coming and she whisked Erika away to help her buy a dress for a date that night, a date she didn't really have. Nadia would actually be with me in a rental car behind the building. I didn't want us to be in either of our cars because I knew Jeremy would recognize them. While they were out, I let Officer Prescott into the building and showed her where she was to hide. I asked her to call me the moment this thing was over which she agreed to do.

I have called Erika and explained to her that I have to go out of town for the night for a medical conference that I thought I would be able to get out of but couldn't. She was a little bit disappointed, but she sounded like she believed me. She had no reason not to believe me.

I really hope this works. I really hope that Jeremy does take the bait, and that he shows his true colors enough to convince Officer Prescott that I'm right about him being her attacker. I also hope that he doesn't act quickly enough that Erika gets hurt before Officer Prescott can stop him. I'm sure it won't come to that. Officer Prescott assured me that at the first sign of Erika being in danger, she would act.

My main worry now is that either Jeremy doesn't show up at all, or that he does show up but acts like a normal, reasonable person and takes no for an answer. Officer Prescott has made it clear to me that she can't hang around at Nadia's place all night and I will have a lot of explaining to do if nothing comes of this and I have to tell Erika that not only did I lie to her about going out of town, but I also installed a police officer in Nadia's bedroom without her knowledge.

Even if Jeremy plays into my hands and acts the way I'm almost certain he will act, Erika might still be pissed off at me about the way I have gone about this. I think it will be a lot easier to make her see this was the only way to do this if I'm proved right about Jeremy though.

I check my watch. It's just after six. I am so tempted to walk around the building and see if I can spot Jeremy lurking around, but I resist the urge. If he spots me, then the whole thing is over before it's even begun. I'll just have to be patient and hope my plan works out. Nadia should be here soon and then at least I'll have someone to talk to so my mind can't get ahead of itself and let me blow everything.

ERIKA

I'm sitting in the living room reading when Nadia comes in wearing the dress we picked out earlier. She does a twirl and smiles.

"You look amazing," I say. "Your date will be putty in your hands."

Nadia smiles, but she looks nervous.

"What is it?" I ask. "You look like you're dreading this."

"I'm just a bit nervous," Nadia says, flashing me a smile that doesn't quite meet her eyes.

"Nadia if you're not comfortable with this, you should just cancel it," I tell her.

"No," she says, shaking her head and smiling again. Her smile looks a bit more real this time. "I'm just being silly."

"Well as long as you're sure," I say. Her nerves are rubbing off on me though and I'm still not convinced she's really not worried about this. "Listen, do you want me to call you in half an hour or so? If things are going well, just ignore my call. If they're not, you can use my call as an excuse to bail. Say there's some sort of emergency or something."

"No, honestly, it's fine," Nadia says. "He's a really nice guy. I'm more nervous in case I say or do something stupid and scare him off."

"There's not much chance of you scaring him off while you're wearing that dress," I laugh.

Nadia laughs and checks her phone.

"Well he's here. I'd best get going," she says.

"Have fun," I tell her.

She smiles and leaves the apartment. I can't help thinking she's not as happy about this date as she's pretending to be. She seemed to be on edge somehow. I know sometimes there can be a few nerves about a date if it's with someone you really like, but that seemed like it was more than that.

I shake my head, shaking the feeling away. Nadia is a grown woman. If she didn't want to go on this date, then she wouldn't be. Still, I make a mental note to text her later on and check in and make sure she's ok.

I go back to my book and I'm soon lost in the pages. I jump when there's a knock on the apartment door. No one has rung the bell. It must be one of Nadia's neighbors. I get up and go to the door. My heart sinks when I pull it open and see Jeremy standing there.

"Hi. How are you?" he says, smiling at me.

"I'm ok. What are you doing here? How did you even get into the building?" I ask.

"I came to see you obviously," he smiles. "Someone was on their way out and they let me in. Aren't you going to invite me in?"

I really don't want to invite him in and I struggle for an excuse. Nadia has barely been gone for five minutes and there's a chance Jeremy saw her leaving so I can't use her as an excuse. And if I tell him Aidan is here, he'll just get mad again.

"Erika?" Jeremy says. "I only want to talk to you."

He smiles reassuringly at me and in the end, I sigh and step back from the door and let him in. I'll hear him out and then tell him I have to go out somewhere. Jeremy moves through to the living room and I follow him, feeling nervous butterflies swimming in my stomach. He's sitting on the couch and he pats the cushion beside him. I pretend not to notice and I take an armchair opposite him.

"So what do you want to talk to me about?" I ask when the silence becomes awkward.

"I don't like the way we left things the last time we talked," Jeremy says. "I just wanted to clear the air between us."

"We're fine Jeremy," I lie, smiling at him, just wanting to convince him we're still friends so he'll leave.

"Good. I'm glad to hear that," Jeremy smiles. "And I want you to know that I get it. I understand why you said we couldn't get back together."

"You do?" I say, surprised and daring to hope he really does finally understand that there's no future in a relationship without any spark in it.

"I do," he smiles. "And I want you to know that you don't need to worry about that. There's no need to be embarrassed because you ended things and then realized you'd made a mistake. We've all made mistakes. We'll just pretend it never happened and move on."

"I …" I start, ready to tell Jeremy he's got it all wrong.

He shakes his head and goes on, not letting me speak.

"It's ok," he says. "I know it's more than that. I know you're afraid we won't go the distance, but this time, we'll do it right Erika."

Before I can decide how to even begin to react to that, Jeremy gets to his feet. He pulls out a small black box from his jeans' pocket and then he drops to one knee. My jaw drops. What the fuck is happening here? How did this escalate so quickly? And how the hell do I get out of it without making him mad?

He opens the box and shows me a beautiful diamond ring.

"Erika, will you marry me?" he says.

His smile is one of triumph. He thinks this is it. That I will say yes and we'll run off into the sunset together. This has gone far enough. I don't know how to make it any clearer to him that we're done here, but I know I have to find a way. I stand up, shaking my head and putting a little bit of distance between Jeremy and me.

"No," I say. "I don't want to be with you Jeremy. And I certainly don't want to marry you."

Jeremy gets up off his knee and snaps the ring box closed, pushing it back into his pocket. He smiles at me.

"Of course you do Erika. I know you. I know you want this. Why won't you just admit it?" he says.

He steps closer to me and I take another step back.

"Are you out of your damned mind?" I say quietly. "Jeremy, this is insane. Even if I wanted to get back with you, we'd only been dating a few months. How do you think proposing to me now is a good idea?"

"How do you not see that we're meant to be together?" Jeremy says, completely ignoring everything I've said to him.

"Because we're not meant to be together. For the last time, I don't want to be with you," I say firmly. "Now please, just leave."

Jeremy shakes his head and a nasty looking grin spreads over his face.

"You really think you can just throw me away like that? Throw us away like that? That you can demand I leave and I'll just go? Well you can't. It doesn't work like that Erika. I have given you every chance to make this right and every time, you have thrown it back in my face. Now I think it's time I taught you a lesson. One you won't forget this time."

He closes the gap between us quickly and although I back away from him again, my back is soon against the wall. I glance to my left and my right, frantically searching for something I can use as a weapon, but there's nothing anywhere near me.

Jeremy has reached me now and he stands with his hands pressed to the wall on either side of me, stopping me from escaping to the side of him.

"You know something Erika? You've just lost your chance to be happy. You've cost me my chance to be happy too and you don't even seem to care about that. Well I care. And if I can't have you, then no one can," he says.

He's so close to me now that I can feel his hot breath on my face with each word. As he speaks, I feel a pain in my head. The pain fades as quickly as it came, but with it comes a flash of memory so vivid it feels like I am living it now.

I see myself in my house, Jeremy in the living room with me, smashing my things, yelling and screaming at me. He is saying those exact words to me; if I can't have you, then no one can. And then his hands are around my throat, squeezing me, choking the life out of me. I am trying to get him off me but he's too strong and I am feeling weaker by the moment as I try to breathe but can't.

It all makes sense now as it all clicks into place. Him turning up at my place right as I was in the middle of grabbing my things after I got out of hospital. He had to have been watching me. It explains his over the top reaction to seeing Aidan in the street that day. It explains why he was so nice to me, trying to get around me and weasel his way back in. And it explains what he meant when he said this time he'll teach me a lesson that I won't forget.

How didn't I see this sooner? I should have put the pieces together sooner than this. And more importantly right now, what the hell do I do to get away from him? Should I pretend I've come around, that I do want him? No, it's too late for that. I can see the anger in his eyes as he stares through me like he's not even seeing me anymore.

He moves his head closer to me and he whispers in my ear.

"I'm going to end you Erika. But first, I'm going to show you just what you're missing out on," he says.

He pulls his head back again and grins at me. I feel my stomach lurching as he moves his face closer to mine. His lips press against mine and I scream as he tries to push his tongue into my mouth. My scream is so muffled by his mouth over mine that it comes out as a sad sounding whimper. There's no way anyone heard that. I lift one knee and try to knee him in the cock, but he blocks my shot with his thigh.

He pulls his mouth away from mine and I can breathe without tasting him again, but my relief at that soon fades and turns to terror when I see the look on Jeremy's face. He is smiling, an ice cold smile that makes my insides shrivel up.

"You want it rough? Then we'll have it rough," he says.

He grabs a handful of my hair and pulls me from the wall, throwing me to the ground. I manage a real scream this time, one I can only pray the neighbors hear and act upon.

"Someone please help me," I yell.

"No one is coming to save you this time Erika. There's no nosy Mr Pritchard to interfere now," Jeremy says as he starts walking towards where I lay on the ground.

I back away, scrambling on my elbows. I jump as a loud voice booms from the direction of the bedrooms.

"Police. Get your hands up."

I glance towards the hallway. Standing in the doorway is Officer Prescott. She isn't messing around. She's standing with her feet apart, braced to move quickly if she needs to.

241

Her hands are out in front of her, the gun she's holding trained on Jeremy. I glance at him. His hands are up and beads of sweat stand out on his forehead.

"You set me up didn't you, you fucking bitch," he says to me.

He doesn't sound angry anymore. He has the sheer audacity to sound hurt, like he's the victim here. I have no idea what he's talking about or how Officer Prescott got into that hallway, but I'm so glad to see her right now. She stopped Jeremy before he could go any further and that's all that matters right now.

"Get down on your knees. Keep your hands where I can see them," Officer Prescott says to Jeremy.

He does as she says, glaring at me the whole time. I scoot further away from him and manage to get to my feet. My legs feel like jelly and I sit down hard on the couch as Officer Prescott moves towards Jeremy. She gets behind him and pulls her handcuffs from her belt, putting her gun back in its holster. She brings Jeremy's hands down behind his back and cuffs him.

"Lie on the ground," she commands. Jeremy doesn't move. "Now."

She yells now and I jump again, but Jeremy complies.

"I'm arresting you on suspicion of assault. You have the right to remain silent, anything you say can and will be used against in a court of law. You have the right to an attorney. If you can't afford one, one will be provided to you. Do you understand what I'm telling you?" Officer Prescott says.

Jeremy nods.

"Yes," he says.

Officer Prescott stands over Jeremy and pulls a radio from her belt.

"We've got him. Get up here and take him to the station," she says.

"Officer?" I say when she puts the radio back on her belt. She glances at me. "I remembered the first attack. When Jeremy grabbed me, it all came back to me. It was him."

"Are you willing to say that in an official statement?" she asks me.

"Yes," I say without hesitation.

"Looks like you're going away for a long time son," Officer Prescott says to Jeremy with a gleeful grin.

Jeremy ignores her and focuses on me.

"Don't you get it Erika? It doesn't have to be this way. Everything I did, I only did because I love you," he says.

"You don't know the meaning of the word love," I snap back at him.

The door to the apartment opens and Officer Moore and another officer come in. They move to Jeremy and take an arm each and pull him to his feet.

"He's been read his rights," Officer Prescott says. "Take him down to the station and get him booked in. See if he wants an attorney and then leave him in a holding cell. I'll follow you guys back, and when I do, Jeremy and I are going to have a little chat."

Officer Moore nods his head and he and the other officer lead Jeremy out of the apartment. Officer Prescott follows them. I hear her speaking but she's stepped out into the hallway and I can't hear what she's saying. After a moment, she comes back in.

"Thank you," I say. "But I don't understand how you were here."

She smiles at me.

"Let's just say you have a guardian angel who forced me to listen," she says.

I frown, more confused than ever. She smiles at me again.

"Are you hurt?" she asks.

I shake my head. My hip is a little tender where I was thrown to the floor, but it doesn't feel like anything more serious than a bruise, and the last thing I want is to end up in the hospital again.

I hear voices coming from the hallway and then the apartment door opens again. Aidan and Nadia burst in and I frown. I am getting more confused by the second, but I am so glad to see Aidan right now.

"I'll let these two explain everything," Officer Prescott says to me. "I need to get down to the station and talk to Jeremy. I'll need you to stop in some time tomorrow and make an official statement. Ok?"

I nod my head and stand up and walk Officer Prescott to the door, ignoring Aidan and Nadia for now. I can only process one thing at a time and even that is hard right now.

"Thank you," I say again as Officer Prescott leaves.

"You're welcome," she smiles.

I watch her walk along the hallway and then I close the door and come back into the living room. I'm am shaking as the reality of what almost happened hits me. Aidan steps forward and wraps me in his arms as my knees start to buckle, and wrapped up in his arms, I feel safe again.

He kisses me hard on the lips and for a moment, I just hold him to me, accepting his kiss. Nadia clears her throat behind me and I pull back from Aidan and smile as I blush.

He leads me to the couch and we sit down side by side.

"I guess I have some explaining to do," he says.

AIDAN

When I got the call from Officer Prescott, I had never felt so relieved in all of my life. She quickly explained that I had been right about everything. Jeremy had tried to attack Erika again, and he was now under arrest. She said that Jeremy's second attack had triggered Erika's memory of the first attack and that Jeremy would definitely be going to prison for what he had done. She was hopeful they could pin attempted murder on him rather than just assault. She told me to come up and see Erika. I didn't need telling twice.

Nadia and I had sprinted into the building and up the stairs as I filled her in on what Officer Prescott had told me. The sight of Erika sitting there, not marked or hurt, had made my heart swell, and I knew in that moment that I loved her.

After she saw Officer Prescott out, she fell into my arms and I kissed her. I wanted to tell her that I loved her now and forever, but I knew that was something I should say in private without Nadia there. I released Erika and we sat down on the couch. I know I have to explain everything to her now and I just have to hope that she understands why I kept things from her and doesn't feel like I betrayed her by keeping her in the dark about all of this until now.

"Twice now Jeremy has threatened me and told me to stay away from you," I say. Erika gasps and I go on before she can start throwing questions at me. "I noticed he had scratches on his hands, the kind he would have gotten from trying to choke someone. I knew he was the one who attacked you, but I had no real evidence of it."

"Why didn't you say something?" Erika asks.

"Be honest Erika. If I had told you my suspicions, would you have believed them to be true, or would you have thought I was just jealous and overreacting."

"Ok, fair point," Erika says with a small smile.

It makes my heart soar to see her smiling.

"So you thought Jeremy had hurt me. And I'm guessing you're the one who set all of this up?" she says.

I nod my head.

"Yes. Jeremy followed me to the hospital today, and this time, he didn't just threaten me. He threatened you too, and that's when I knew I had to make sure he didn't get away with this. I told Jeremy I was going out of town tonight and to stay away from you, knowing he would take the bait. Then I convinced Nadia to help me by getting you out of the house this afternoon so that Officer Prescott could sneak in. I told Officer Prescott everything. She was skeptical at first, but she agreed to be here. And the rest, as they say, is history."

Erika is quiet for a moment and then she glances at Nadia.

"That's why you seemed so nervous before you went out wasn't it? You didn't really have a date," Erika says to Nadia.

Nadia nods.

"Yes. I'm sorry I lied to you," she says.

"I'm sorry about that too," I say.

"I understand why you didn't tell me at first, but why didn't you tell me about the plan for tonight? Even if I thought you were jealous, I would have come around when you told me you'd even managed to convince the police about this," Erika says.

"I wanted to tell you, but I figured if I was wrong, I didn't want to scare you half to death for no reason. And if I was right, for this to work, you needed to act natural around Jeremy. If you were too much on edge or acting like you were scared of him before he even started with the threats, then he would have known something was up and he would have walked away from this without being punished. There's no way I could have convinced Officer Prescott that Jeremy was the one who attacked you if he had come here tonight and not caused a scene."

"He asked me to marry him before he started actin all crazy," Erika says.

"Wow, I knew he was crazy, but that's a step too far even for him," I say.

Erika laughs and nudges me with her elbow.

"Are you saying someone would have to be crazy to want to marry me?" she laughs.

"No of course not," I say quickly. "But it's a big step from someone you're not even seeing."

"It was pretty intense," Erika admits. "I was really scared for a while there, but I'm glad it's all over now."

"You don't have to be scared ever again," I tell her. "Jeremy is in custody now and I swear I won't let him or anyone else hurt you ever again."

She smiles at me and I see tears shining on the surface of her eyes. I reach out and squeeze her hand and she squeezes back.

"Can you forgive me for keeping this from you?" I ask.

She nods her head and smiles at me.

"Yes. But don't make a habit out of it ok? I don't want you to think I can't handle stuff alright?"

"Noted," I smile.

Nadia stands up.

"I'm going to go and make some tea," she says. "Erika has had quite a shock tonight and it will do her good. And I can see you two are just dying for me to leave the room so you can get back to kissing."

Erika blushes again and Nadia laughs as she heads out of the room.

"Don't worry. I'll give a big cough when I'm coming back," she says.

She's barely out of the door when I kiss Erika again. Her arms wrap around me and we hold each other tightly as we kiss. For all Erika's touch, her kiss, has its usual effect on me, the kiss isn't a passionate kiss. It's a sensual kiss, a tender kiss. A kiss that I hope tells Erika that I never want to let her go again, and a kiss that I hope is her way of telling me that she's not going anywhere. I pull back after a couple of minutes and look into Erika's eyes.

"I know this is too soon, but I also know how close I came to losing you. If Jeremy had gotten to you without Officer Prescott being around …"

"It's ok," Erika says. "I'm ok."

"I know," I smile. "But it made me realize something. And I don't care that it's too soon to say it. Erika, I love you."

"I love you too," she says.

Her eyes fill with tears again and she smiles as they start to fall.

"They're happy tears this time," she tells me.

We kiss again. She tastes of her salty tears. I hold her tightly against me, like I'm afraid that she'll float away if I let go of her. The truth is, I'm so happy to hear Erika saying those words back to me, that I think I might float away at any given minute. When the kiss ends, I take Erika's hand in mine and look at her again.

"I know this is probably a stupid question after we've already told each other we love each other, but will you be my girl-friend Erika?"

She nods her head and I relax slightly. I'm not going to lose her. I'm going to do everything in my power to make her happy and make sure that never happens.

"I haven't so much as looked at anyone else since you came into my life, but I want to make it official. We're exclusive right?"

"Right," Erika laughs. Her laugh fades but she's still smiling. "You know, I never thought I would be grateful to the guy that almost killed me, but if that hadn't have happened we never would have met."

"I'd like to think we still would have met. That fate would have found a way to bring us together," I smile.

Erika smiles back at me and I lean in for another kiss, but before our lips touch, Nadia coughs loudly from the hallway. We move apart and Nadia comes into the room. She is carrying a tray with a teapot, a milk jug, a sugar bowl and two cups. I frown at the two cups.

"There are three of us Nadia," I say.

"Haven't you heard the saying; three's a crowd?" Nadia says. "I wanted to see you and make sure you were ok Erika, but I'm going out now."

"Don't be silly. I don't want you to feel like you're not welcome in your own home," Erika says.

"You're not making me feel like that at all," Nadia says, waving her hand. "Remember the guy I told you about from the gym?"

Its news to me but Erika nods and sits forward on the couch.

"It went well the other night with him?" she asks.

"Really well," Nadia grins. "It seemed a shame to get all dressed up like this and not go out, so I called him from the kitchen and we're going out for dinner. We'll probably do something else afterwards. So don't wait up ok?"

Nadia winks and I cringe.

"God Nadia, leave something to the imagination," I say.

She laughs and shakes her head.

"Oh don't be such a prude," she chastises me.

Her phone dings and she pulls it out of her hand bag and looks at the screen.

"That's him," she says. "Have fun you two."

"You too," Erika calls after her.

We turn to face each other as the door closes behind Nadia, and this time when we kiss, we don't jump apart. We stayed wrapped in each other's arms, the tea forgotten, everything forgotten except each other.

Erika

My stomach is rolling with nerves and I run to the bathroom and grab a piece of tissue to wipe my palms dry. I hear laughter from the room I left and I go back.

"It's not funny. I'm shitting a brick here," I tell Nadia who is still laughing.

"Well yeah, it's natural to be nervous," she says. She narrows her eyes and stops laughing for a moment. "You're not having second thoughts are you? You can tell me if you are."

"I'm not," I tell her. "I want to marry Aidan more than anything. It's not the thought of marrying him that's got me this way. It's the thought of walking down the aisle in front of all of those people. What if I trip and fall over or something?"

Nadia is laughing again when she replies.

"Well it'll give all of your guests a fantastic story to tell their friends," she says.

"That's not helping," I groan.

She laughs again and gets up off the chair and comes to my side. She moves in front of me and takes both of my hands in both of hers.

"Listen to me. You're not going to fall. You're going to walk down the aisle and the only thing anyone will be telling their friends after this is over is how beautiful you looked. Everything is going to be fine Erika," she says. "Just try to relax and enjoy your day."

"Thank you," I tell her. I feel a little bit better at her words. She's right. Everything will be fine. I'm just worrying about nothing. "And thank you for being here with me, keeping me calm."

"Where else would I be?" Nadia asks. "Aidan might have gained a wife, but I've gained a best friend."

I pull her in for a hug, careful not to wrinkle either of our dresses.

"Now come on, let's get moving," Nadia says, stepping back. "Jennifer is going to string me up if I don't get you downstairs on time."

I pick up my bouquet and take one last look in the mirror. My dress fits like a glove. It's strapless and long, a straight white satin gown. I feel like a character in a fairy tale wearing it. I follow Nadia out of the room and to the elevator. A few of the hotel guests smile as we pass them. I smile back, so happy to finally be about to marry the man of my dreams.

We go down in the elevator and move through the lobby to the ballroom where our ceremony will take place. After the ceremony, we'll go to the dining room for a meal and the staff will come in and transform the ballroom, moving the furniture out of the way and set up for dancing at our reception.

Jennifer smiles when she sees me approaching. She's wearing a lilac dress that matches Nadia's. Jennifer is my Matron of Honor and Nadia is my Maid of Honor and they will be walking me down the aisle as my parents couldn't make the wedding. I was upset when I heard they couldn't come, but I remind myself they're happy for me and I'm not going to let that ruin my day.

"Are you ready?" Jennifer asks me.

"Yeah," I say.

"Actually, you're not quite ready," she says.

She and Nadia share a smile and I frown, confused. A door opens to my side and my jaw drops as my dad steps out dressed in a black tuxedo.

"Dad? What are you doing here?" I ask.

"As if we would miss your wedding," he laughs. "We wanted to surprise you."

"Well you've certainly done that," I laugh as I hug him.

The wedding march begins to play from inside of the ballroom. Jennifer and Nadia pull the doors open and begin to walk down the aisle. My dad offers me his arm and I take it and we walk down the aisle, walking towards my future with my one true love.

As soon as I see Aidan standing at the front of the ballroom looking gorgeous in his tuxedo that matches my dad's, I feel my nerves melting away replaced with the happiest feeling I have ever felt. I have nothing to be nervous about. I know that this is the first day of the rest of my life, and it's a life I never even dared to dream I could have and now it's mine.

THE END

RECKLESS ENTANGLEMENT

Chapter 1
Callie

I hurry across the parking lot, coming as close as I can to running without risking breaking an ankle. My skin tight pencil skirt and killer heels aren't the kind of outfit a girl runs in. They aren't the sort of outfit I ever pictured myself waitressing in either, but that's the joy of working in La Trattoria. I can't complain though. It's high end enough that the tips from my part time job pay my bills and leave me with enough time to study for college.

I check my watch as I burst through the back door and into the staff room, a grubby room filled with a scratched table and three broken chairs. A stark contrast to the restaurant floor where everything is immaculate, brand new and shiny.

My heart sinks when I see Marco sitting in one of the chairs, his feet propped up on the table. As bosses go, he's the worst.

He's by far the laziest man I've ever met, but his standards rival those of The Waldorf when it comes to us waitresses. He makes a show of looking at his watch. He tuts and shakes his head.

"I'm sorry," I say, already taking my coat off. "There was an accident on the way in and the diversion was crazy busy. I'll make the time up I swear."

"See that you do Callie." He gets up and saunters towards the door, blocking my path as I try to leave the room. "This is just unprofessional. I guess I shouldn't expect better from a student though, huh?"

With that, he's gone, leaving me standing there open mouthed at the sheer audacity of him calling me unprofessional. All of this drama because I was two minutes late. Like *literally* two minutes. It's not really about me being a few minutes late though. It's about me rejecting his advances last week when he hit on me in his office.

As if I could ever be attracted to him. I mean he's not ugly or anything to look at, but boy is he ugly on the inside. Besides, sleeping with the boss is such a cliché, and I refuse to be one of those girls who is never quite sure if she's kept around because she's good at her job, or because she's eye candy for the boss.

I shake my head, telling myself to let it go. I won't let that douchebag into my head. I hit the restaurant floor with my fake smile plastered on.

"Callie? Table three is up," the line chef shouts the second I appear.

I rush forward and grab the two plates. They're hot, burning my skin and I almost let them go, but I manage to hold onto them. I'm used to being burned by the plates, but the first time each night always gets me. I rush them to the table, slowing down at the last second and smiling once more. "One carbonara?" I say.

The woman at the table smiles and gestures that it's hers.

I set the plate down in front of her and turn to the man. "And one lasagna." I smile, placing the plate down in front of him. "Enjoy your meals."

They thank me, but as I walk away, I can hear them muttering under their breath about how long it's taken. Great. That's hardly my fault, I wasn't even here when their order was taken, but it'll be me who gets stiffed on the tip.

As I rush back to the counter, Marco catches up with me. "Table three are not impressed with your service Callie, and frankly, neither am I. Get it together or you're done here," he says.

I bite my tongue, determined not to let him get to me. He knows that order being late wasn't my fault. Sasha, one of the other waitresses catches my eye and pulls a face behind Marco's back, making me feel slightly better about the whole thing.

I reach the counter and collect the next order, a single pizza. I turn around to deliver it and find Marco once more blocking my path.

"Are you ignoring me?" he demands.

"No," I say, nodding towards the plate in my hand. "Just trying to get us caught up."

"Maybe we wouldn't be in the weeds if you had shown up on time," he says, but he moves out of my way.

I can feel my temperature rising in anger at his tone of voice as I rush across the restaurant. My focus is on trying not to show my anger, and I'm not paying as much attention as I should be to the restaurant floor. Before I register what's happening, I feel myself tripping.

I start to fall and everything slows down as my stomach turns over. I have time to imagine the clatter as I slam to the ground, the laughter, Marco's anger that I've wasted the pizza. As if by a miraculous intervention warm hands catch the tops of my arms saving both me and the pizza from taking a dive.

I look up to thank my savior but the words die on my lips as I take in the tousled rich brown hair, the square jaw, and the deep chocolate eyes I could easily lose myself in. I swallow hard, dragging my eyes away hurriedly as I feel my cheeks turning red. My eyes move downwards of their own accord, taking in a black shirt covering huge pecs and abs of steel.

My stomach rolls again, but this time it's nothing to do with me falling. It's him. His hands are still on me and I can feel him watching me. I look back up to his face and once more I am assaulted by his eyes.

"For God's sake take the pizza to the damned customer," Marco hisses in my ear.

The moment is broken and the man pulls his hands away from me, although he still holds my gaze with his own. I try to thank him, but my voice is gone and I just scurry away, thanking my lucky stars that the table is one of the ones in the patio area.

The cool night air washes over me as I go outside and I feel the flush in my cheeks start to die down. I deliver the pizza uneventfully and take a moment to just breathe in a few deep breaths. I steel myself for Marco's tirade and head back inside.

A woman practically runs towards me when she sees me come back in. "I'm so sorry miss," she says. "Are you ok?"

"I-I'm fine," I say with no idea who she is or what's going on.

She sees confusion written all over my face and she smiles sheepishly. "It was my bag you tripped over," she explains.

"Oh," I say, forcing a soft laugh. "Don't worry about it. Really, I should have been watching where I was going." I excuse myself as soon as I can without looking rude and make my way back towards the counter.

"Chef wants you to go and grab some ice from out back," Sasha says as I approach.

I nod, glad for the chance to get off the floor and take a moment to compose myself. I've been here less than half an hour and my shift is already spiraling. I hurry out the back and I spot him again. The man who saved me. He's talking to Marco and my heart sinks for a moment. Is he complaining about me?

I realize with a start the shirt he's wearing isn't any old black shirt. It's one of ours. He must have started working here tonight. Great. So I have to see him every time I'm working now.

I've allowed myself to become distracted again, and as I walk, I kick a trash can, hurting my toes so badly I curse out loud before I can stop myself.

Marco and the hot guy both turn in my direction, but Marco might as well not be there. The guy's eyes are on mine again, and I can see the lust in them. It's like his eyes are burning through my clothes, stripping me naked.

I feel myself get wet at the thought of where his hands might go, where his tongue might go. I want to look away, but I can't. I am getting flustered, my skin flushing again, my heart racing and my palms sweating. He winks at me, a wink that sends a shiver through my body, and then he breaks eye contact and I can move again, think again.

"Callie, get over here," Marco shouts.

Oh, wonderful. Now he's going to embarrass me in front of the hot guy. Reluctantly, I head over. "Chef needs some ice," I explain.

"Chef can wait a moment," Marco says. "I want to introduce you to Matt. He's just transferred here from another branch. I want you to show him around, make him feel welcome. If that's not too much trouble." He walks away without another word.

I shake my head. "Asshole," I mutter under my breath.

"I hope you mean him and not me." Matt grins.

I nod, confirming it to be the case, but I'm not so sure I'm not talking about both of them. Matt is hot and there's no denying the effect he has on me, but no one should be this cool and arrogant on their first night in a new job.

Something tells me Matt is going to be trouble and I vow then and there that I will keep my distance from him. I'll show him the ropes, but that's it. I'll be cool and professional and leave it at that. I can do that. I can.

Chapter Two
Matt

"The break room and restroom is that way, and as you know the restaurant floor is that way," Callie says, pointing first one way and then the other.

I nod, watching her with amusement as she tries and fails to keep her eyes off my chest. I guess I'm not one to talk. From the moment she fell into my arms, I knew there was something special about her.

For starters, she's beautiful. Her eyes are a stunning, vivid green, the color of emeralds. Her skin is flawless and I want to reach out and run my fingers down her cheek. Her long gold-brown hair is pulled back into a high ponytail, but I can see how long it is and I can't help but imagine her pulling it loose, imagine myself pushing my hands into it, pulling her closer to me. My cock is getting hard just thinking about what I could do to this gorgeous creature.

I allow my eyes to move lower, taking in her full breasts, the curve of her hips. She sure knows how to rock this uniform like no one I've ever met.

She clears her throat and I know she's caught me staring. That makes two of us then. I meet her eyes and smile at her. "And my tour is over?" I say.

"I'm sorry. I have a lot to do. No offense Matt, but if you need hand holding, you're not going to last two minutes here," she says.

"Got it," I say, pushing myself up from the wall I've been leaning on. "Thank you for making me feel so welcome." I walk away, heading for the restaurant floor, grinning to myself. I don't need to look back to know that Callie is watching me walk away, her jaw hanging open in shock.

She's made it clear to me that her plan is to avoid contact with me as much as possible. It should raise my suspicions, yet strangely, it doesn't. I'm not blind. I saw the way she was looking at me. And I have a feeling that's why she wants to avoid me. Maybe she's one of those girls who don't date colleagues.

In one sense, I'm upset that Callie doesn't want to be around me. I would be more than happy to have her around me all day, every day. But in another sense, I think it's a good thing, because I can't allow my focus to slip, and at least this way, I don't have to be the one to push her away.

I'm here for one reason and one reason only, and that reason is too important to spend my time flirting with Callie. I came here to do what needs to be done. Not to make friends, and most certainly not to fall for one of the waitresses.

I'll play along with Callie's avoidance of me. That way, I can't become distracted from the real reason I'm here.

Please Pre-order Here:
Reckless Entanglement

ABOUT THE AUTHOR

Thank you so much for reading!
If you have enjoyed the book and would like to leave a
precious review for me, please kindly do so here.

Crushing on My Doctor

Please click on the link below to receive info about my latest
releases and giveaways.
NEVER MISS A THING

Or
come and say hello here:

ALSO BY IONA ROSE

Nanny Wanted

CEO's Secret Baby

New Boss, Old Enemy

Craving The CEO

Forbidden Touch

Printed in Great Britain
by Amazon